COMFORT
and Joy

COMFORT *and Joy*

Gerald Cole

Based on the screenplay by Bill Forsyth

Methuen

A Methuen Paperback

COMFORT AND JOY
ISBN 0 413 55390 6

First published in 1984
by Methuen London Ltd
11 New Fetter Lane, London EC4P 4EE

Set in IBM 11 point Baskerville by Tek-Art, Croydon, Surrey
Printed in Great Britain by
Richard Clay (The Chaucer Press) Ltd,
Bungay, Suffolk

'In cities, mutinies; in countries, discord; in palaces, treason; and the bond cracked twixt son and father. Ruinous disorders follow us disquietly to our graves.'

William Shakespeare

'There are times when the most practical thing is to lie down.'

Saul Bellow

To Thomas

1

Sunday

'It's a bit of a shock, Maddy'

'God help us –'

The words squeezed through Alan Bird's lips as the tall, slim, strawberry blonde eased the cashmere scarf from counter to voluminous coat pocket, pirouetting as she did it to smile sweetly at the unheeding security guard at her elbow. Dazzled by this unexpected attention, the man broke into a hesitant smile.

From his vantage point at the further end of the counter, Alan sighed deeply. The gall of the woman was boundless. That was her third scarf now – not to mention the dozen lace handkerchiefs, four silk slips, two pairs of Bally shoes and enough Christmas tree lights to illuminate the Kelvin Hall, which were already packed into the deep calf leather bag hanging from her shoulder – a bag she did not have with her when she had entered the store half an hour before. So far she had paid only for the final set of lights.

Abruptly she was gone, drifting quietly but purposefully through the pre-Christmas crush. As inconspicuous as any attractive, elegantly attired young woman in Glasgow's premier department store.

Alan, who had been picking idly at a spotted pink cravat, abandoned it and set off in pursuit. A stocky, scurrying, worried-looking man in his mid-thirties, he maintained a discreet distance, glancing away when the young woman looked back, eyeing her casually as she circled through menswear and glassware and into haberdashery.

At least she was easy to watch. There was a delicacy about her movements at odds with her armour of sophistication, the suggestion of a teasing vulnerability. A sheer joy, too, in the act of theft that belied any air of coolness. She was on a private high. Alan could see it in the flash of her large, dark eyes. A thrill as secret and as heady as sex.

He snatched up a small glass lion and pretended to study it as the girl paused among a forest of dangling handbags. An evening bag was popped into a clutch bag, the clutch bag into a large handbag. While Alan winced at the blatancy of it, the girl took the handbag to the sales counter.

'Don't bother to wrap it,' she heard her tell the assistant. 'I'll be using it straightaway.'

She paid, and, with a silky smile, angled away into the main hall, aiming directly for the street doors. For all its appearance of casualness, her speed was surprising.

Alan pushed the glass animal awkwardly back into its display and hurried after her. She was through the main doors before he had cleared the crowd milling at the foot of the oak stairway rising to the first floor.

Outside, shoppers thronged the pedestrianized precinct of Buchanan Street. Shop windows and festive displays glowed in the gathering dusk. Alan glimpsed the girl sidling through a cluster of orange-haired punks. She was heading for Argyle Street, the St Enoch Square underground station.

A dozen swift steps took him to her side. She walked quickly, confidently, her chin lifted, her cheeks flushed with the crisp December air – and success. He reached out and clasped her arm.

'You'll be the death of me, Maddy,' he murmured.

Her pace did not slacken; he was almost running to keep up with her.

'Shut up and get the car.' She glanced at his scalp as he bobbed level with her. In her high heels their heights were similar. 'You're going bald, did you know? It must be nerves.'

'Oh, thank you.'

Laughter bubbled into her throat as he finally dared a covert glance over his shoulder. They were at the corner of Argyle Street. No burly store detective was bearing down on them. They had got away with it. Or rather, Maddy had. Again.

Alan let go a shuddering sigh, which had little to do with relief. He was sighing a lot these days.

'I got some more Christmas lights for you,' Maddy offered.

When he glanced at her, she was already looking

away, the light of mischief in her eyes.

He closed his seat belt, twisted the BMW's ignition and slipped into first, noticing, as he looked to the rear, that Maddy's belt was still unclipped. She was too busy poring over her new acquisitions.

He stifled a reprimand. No, if he were going to nag her, the larger misdemeanour would be a better subject. He frowned and pulled away from the kerb, annoyed that he was annoyed, grudgingly resentful of Maddy for having forced him once more into the role of a nag. It didn't fit his image of himself. Silver-tongued radio DJs driving pale red BMW 323i Cabriolets didn't carp about seat belts. (He wasn't so sure about kleptomania.) Worse, it didn't fit his image of the relationship.

Maddy was pushing him. He could see it in the self-congratulatory way she studied each stolen item, knowing his disapproval, actively courting it . . . A small, spiteful, wounding need, tearing at the fabric of their intimacy. He forgave her, because he found it easy, but it made no sense to him.

He'd enjoyed it far more when they had argued. Fierce, blistering, furniture-throwing rows that invariably ended in slammed front doors and long, solitary drives through the night – even if he had felt like death in the studio next morning. But he'd coped with all that. Rows cleared the air wonderfully. The fact that they could be survived only confirmed the couple's closeness; the fact that they might not be added masochistic spice to the reconciliations.

It was only as the rows had abated that it had occurred to Alan that that kind of loving warfare was more appropriate to eighteen-year-olds than a couple aged thirty-seven and twenty-seven. He'd rather hoped that Maddy had come to a similar conclusion.

'Shit!' She pulled a silk slip closer to the windscreen, brushing the wheel with its edge. 'These are all size fourteen!'

'You've got to stop it, Maddy,' Alan told her. 'I can't take the strain.'

'Stay home then.'

Her glibness defeated him. He tried sweet reason. 'If you're going to steal things then at least be practical. We needed onions. We did not need more Christmas lights . . .'

'You buy the food.' Maddy rummaged in her shoulder bag. 'I'll get the goodies.'

Alan was too busy controlling his exasperation to notice the long, slim packet of cigarillos she had unearthed. She put one between her lips and struggled to light it. The lighter did catch Alan's eye. It was something he hadn't seen her acquire – a foot-long gaudily ornamented pedestal, apparently made of solid silver.

'Please, don't smoke in the car, Maddy.'

He almost bit off the words as he said them, hearing the moan in his own voice. Maddy's glance was suddenly tender, as if she sympathized with his dilemma, but could do nothing about it. She took a deep, self-conscious draw on the cigarillo, then stretched out an arm and traced a finger round the curve of his ear. Alan's mouth tightened as she began to stroke his hair. Her lips formed into a smile. Under its brilliance the tension began to ease from Alan's jawline. Maddy hummed softly, her smile broadening as Alan glanced at her.

He shook his head, struggling to maintain his exasperation. It was a battle he had lost long, long ago.

'God help us –' he murmured.

Redbrick and tall, the apartment block reared itself from the shoulder of a fashionable hill in Langside, down whose flanks Mary Queen of Scots' supporters had once poured in ungainly rout. Where they'd got their breath back, and their feet wet, in a small stream at the bottom, a railway bridge now crossed the Kilmarnock Road. The picture window of Alan's rooftop apartment provided a panoramic view, but as Maddy closed the curtains only street lamps and lighted windows were visible, all the way to the low, surrounding hills.

Propped against the sofa, his legs stretched across the all-wool Berber, Alan watched her pass, exchanging a quiet smile. Peace was declared. The aberrations of the afternoon forgotten, at least until the next time, which might be a good two months away. Alan preferred not to think about that.

Festooned with Christmas lights, he used a screwdriver to repair a faulty connection. At intervals he looked up to catch Maddy ferrying her 'goodies' in from the hall. She was, he decided, the most attractive woman he had ever known.

Not the most beautiful, though she was stunning enough; he found something glacial in physical perfection. Maddy was too lively for that, too feminine, too downright bitchy when the mood took her. And much, much too sexy.

It was a sexiness that manifested itself not just in bed, or in the hothouse media milieu where they'd met, but in the quietest, most mundane domestic situations. The way she dressed so elegantly but with such casual speed. The way she thumped a pillow, or picked up a phone.

It was something it had taken him four tempestuous years to appreciate.

'What do you think of the handbags?' she interrupted his thoughts, plomping on to the sofa and nudging his shoulder with a shapely knee. She spread her three new acquisitions across the cushions.

Alan turned his head to look. 'Lovely . . . the only problem is we've got fifty like them in the wardrobe.'

'Oh, you can never have too many handbags. Anyway, these are for presents.'

'That's an idea.' Alan nodded at the largest. 'Just right for Aunty Betty. About her size . . .'

'How rude –' Maddy sounded unconvincing. Her aunt was a small, round woman from Pollockshields, barely five feet tall and fractionally wider. 'What do you think of these scarves, then?' She held them up for him.

'I like the blue one.'

'Twenty-three pounds fifty pee. But to you –' She presented it to him. He accepted it with his free hand, making the coloured bulbs jingle across his chest.

'Now why the four sets of lights?' he asked.

'I want to have lots of lights on the tree.'

He glanced in the corner where the bulb-bedecked tree was already threatening to engulf the stereo rack. 'We can always use the other two sets as spares.'

'No!' Her response was so sharp he looked at her. 'No, they all go on the tree.'

'Okay.' He was more than happy to be conciliatory.

He went back to his repairs while Maddy picked through her acquisitions. There was something desultory about her movements. After a pause, he asked, 'Want to go out tonight?'

'No.'

She sounded vague.

'Do you want to eat?'

'Later.'

Her voice had softened; her knee increased its pressure on his shoulder.

With a suspicious smile, Alan put down his screwdriver. He turned but Maddy's head was down, her face hidden in a swathe of hair.

'Do you want to wrap Aunty Betty's handbag?' he suggested, reaching up to smooth back the long ruddy blonde strands.

She pecked suddenly at his hand, like some small supplicating animal. 'No,' she whispered.

He laughed as her knees buckled and she slid down from the sofa, into his encircling arm. He glimpsed the white flash of her teeth, then they began to kiss, softly, easily, sweetly at first. Then with increasing urgency until they were easing sideways on to the Berber.

Abruptly the lights draped over Alan's upper half began to flash on and off, like so many miniaturized hazard warnings. The couple broke apart with a surprised laugh. Then, gingerly, Maddy helped Alan extricate himself.

There was a fierceness in her lovemaking that surprised almost as much as it delighted him. Maddy had never been inhibited in that regard, in any way – their nights seemed to be filled equally with breathless passion and manic giggling. But tonight was different. Alan felt *devoured*, as if he'd received the benefit of several weeks' pent-up affection, or possibly a bountiful apology for the afternoon's misdemeanours. Dazed, and very grateful, he found his second sock mysteriously behind the sofa, and hobbled through to the kitchen to prepare a meal.

Maddy had taught him to cook shortly after they had moved in. Not because she knew anything about cooking. She didn't. There were simply those who cooked well and those who ate well; it was very difficult to be both; she had explained it very carefully. Maddy, quite plainly, liked to eat well.

Consequently tonight Alan made a special effort with some spaghetti bolognaise and they finished a half bottle of red at the kitchen table.

Afterwards, feeling rosy and replete, Alan wandered back into the living room. He picked up the Christmas lights, which seemed to have survived the carpet wrestling intact, deposited them next to the tree and then spotted a book he had been reading lying on a shelf of the rack system. Opening it, he sank into an armchair. The book was Maddy's, a torrid romance in which he had become embroiled against his better judgment. It trapped him again and five minutes evaporated before he realized that Maddy had not joined him.

Plates clattered in the kitchen. He glanced up at her outline through the frosted-glass partition.

'You're sure you don't want to go out, Maddy?' he called. 'It's only eight.'

'No –'

She seemed distracted.

He looked back at his book, only faintly curious, glad not to have to shatter the intimacy of the evening.

A moment later Maddy came in. She was carrying a cardboard box and a bundle of newspapers. She put the box on the sofa and began taking objects off the mantelpiece, wrapping some in the newspaper, piling them inside.

Alan observed her in occasional upward glances from his page. He said nothing. Wilder urges than mantel ornament rearrangement had seized Maddy before. It wasn't particularly convenient, but it wasn't especially unusual either.

But, as he watched, her activities spread, became more purposeful. She emptied the bookshelf in the alcove next to the mantelshelf, standing the books in neat piles on the carpet. She picked up a china lamp from the coffee table, unplugged its lead and wrapped it around the base. She reached for two of Alan's favourite reproductions hanging over the sofa . . .

Alan put down his book. 'Maddy, what are you up to?'

She wrapped both pictures carefully before she replied.

'I'm leaving, Alan. I'm taking some things – my things – and I'm leaving.'

Alan blinked. In an awful, rushing silence he felt a string tighten in his stomach, squeezing his innards, drawing them down into his bowels.

Maddy looked at him. 'I have to go. I meant to tell you, but the moment didn't arise. I wanted to talk to you about it, but it just didn't happen . . .'

The words petered out. She pushed the pictures quickly into the cardboard box. She began snatching cushions off the sofa.

'Maddy, please,' Alan gasped. 'Sit down – we can talk about it now –'

She shook her head. 'It's too late – George is coming over soon – he's hired a truck. I meant to tell you ages ago –'

Alan's mind raced. Out of the suddenly crumbling edifice of his life he grabbed at something. 'Your sister set this up, didn't she? It's your crazy sister!'

Maddy's sister lived in Paisley with two children and a husband who installed beer pumps. She did not approve of unwedded bliss.

'No! It's *me* – *I'm* doing it.' The anguish in Maddy's voice startled and appalled Alan. She took a breather. 'I asked George to help me move out, that's all.'

They stared at each other across gulfs Alan had only dimly realized, or thought easily bridgeable. The doorbell saved Maddy's obvious embarrassment.

While she went to the door, Alan remained rooted in the armchair, gripping his book. Things were happening too fast; he needed time to think, to marshal his arguments. Voices sounded in the hallway. Two brown-coated removal men – one pimply, one middle-aged – entered the living room. They nooded cheerily at Alan. George, Maddy's brother-in-law, hovered sheepishly in the background.

Maddy bustled past them and told the removal men to start with the kitchen table.

As they disappeared into the kitchen, Alan said loudly, 'You're quite serious about this then, Maddy?'

Before she could reply, the removal men reappeared with the table and carried it out into the hallway. To make room for them, George was forced to move in front of Alan's chair.

'I'm really sorry about this, Alan.' He shuffled his feet apologetically. 'I'm just helping out. No hard feelings, eh? It's just – you know – women . . .' A half smile withered under Alan's bemused gaze.

'George,' Maddy broke in, 'there are some chairs in the kitchen . . .'

Nodding gratefully, George made his exit.

Order was returning to Alan's mind. He wasn't bemused anymore. He was panic-stricken.

'Maddy, baby,' he cried. 'Please talk to me – please stay and *talk* to me!'

Maddy's gaze softened. 'Don't let's drag it out, Alan. Don't be cruel . . .'

There was a note of special pleading in her

voice which subtly shifted the blame for the upheaval on to him. Instantly he was bemused again.

Maddy picked up the carboard box from the sofa and swept out. The middle-aged removal man passed her at the door. 'Nice chair,' he commented, smiling at where Alan sat. Alan nodded dully, and then realized what the man meant. He mumbled an apology and got up.

He paused a moment, and dived for the door. The pimply removal man and a colleague he hadn't seen before were manoeuvring a large wardrobe out on to the landing. Alan squeezed past and caught up with Maddy halfway down the first flight.

'Maddy!'

She turned, bristling. 'Please stop this, Alan! You're not making it easy. You don't make anything easy!'

Abruptly she clattered away down the steps. Alan gaped after her. What did she mean, *easy*? Shoplifting? Everyday living? Sex . . .?

The pimply removal man trod on his instep and apologized profusely. The wardrobe had caught up with him.

Alan went back into the flat. He passed George with an armful of chairs, and two more removal men with his armchair. He glanced in the bedroom. There were two tea chests at the end of the bed, already almost full.

The place was changing even as he looked at it; his whole life was being dismantled under his very eyes.

He wandered into the living room. Another tea chest had materialized. As he peered into it, the middle-aged removal man appeared behind him and spotted Alan's book on the carpet. He clicked his tongue and picked it up.

'Right – just leave the book –' Alan stuttered. 'I'm reading it – leave it, all right –'

The man hesitated as Maddy came in.

'Put it in the box, please. It's my book,' she reminded Alan.

'I'm halfway through it!' he exploded. 'Couldn't you just leave the damned book?'

'You didn't buy it –'

'Neither did you!'

'Well, it's mine.'

'Right! Right!' He felt himself shaking. 'Well, that's my sweater, if it comes down to it. So – give me the sweater –'

Maddy sighed. 'You're upset. Don't be childish.'

'If I'm a child, then you're a thief!' Alan stuck out his hand. 'Give me the sweater.'

Maddy sighed again. Then, quickly, she took hold of the garment, shrugged it over her head and pushed it into Alan's hands. 'I only wanted it as a keepsake, but if you feel that strongly about it you can have it.'

He gazed at it, momentarily nonplussed.

'Have the book too.' She snatched it from the removal man, who had been following the exchange with only mild interest, but who now gazed with undisguised admiration at Maddy's well filled bra. 'With my compliments –'

She turned on her heel and went into the bedroom. The removal man raised appreciative eyebrows.

Experts were taking his life apart, stripping the flat like brown-coated locusts. Vast areas of strangely imprinted carpet began to surface, splashes of blank, magnolia-painted walls he couldn't remember seeing before. The pace was so rapid it took on a surreal quality.

It was George who blushingly asked Alan to help him manhandle the dressing-table out of the bedroom.

'I don't want to do this. I don't know why I'm doing this . . .' A mumbled litany of protest accompanied their progress into the hallway. 'It's very good of you, Alan . . . very good of you . . . just a bit down on your side . . . watch the handle . . .'

Suddenly Maddy was there, alone in the kitchen doorway, wrapped in a fur coat and cradling an alabaster bust of Michelangelo's David, unwittingly donated by an Argyle Street travel agent.

'Let's talk it over, eh?' Alan suggested quietly.

Maddy sighed. 'We've been talking it over for four years –'

They became disconcertingly aware of the middle-aged removal man hovering at Alan's elbow and eyeing Maddy's coat as though wondering if Alan were about to demand that as well as the sweater. If the man had known the evening was going to include an impromptu striptease he wouldn't have quibbled so much about the rate. 'Oh – is the washing machine to go?' he asked.

'No – no, that stays.'

Alan and Maddy spoke together, a last gesture of domestic unity.

As the man went, Maddy moved fractionally closer. 'Don't do anything foolish, don't try to contact me . . .' Her voice was almost tender. 'You keep the gramophone, okay?'

Alan nodded faintly. 'Whoopee . . .' he murmured. He risked the glum ghost of a smile.

Still clutching the bust, Maddy waited beside him in the cold street while George and the removal men tied down the furniture inside a large pantechnicon. She was quiet, giving him – he realized – the space to make a farewell declaration. It was a speech he had not rehearsed, had never dreamed he would have to make. He floundered.

'You really, *really* want to leave then? You really want to go . . . now . . . leave . . . ?'

The pantechnicon's doors thumped shut. Whistling, the removal men retreated to the cab.

'Yes,' Maddy admitted.

Alan puffed his cheeks, as though astonished at her blatancy. But her blatancy had always astonished – and intrigued him. The gesture was as much to hide a renewed bout of trembling. 'It's a bit of a shock.'

'I know,' Maddy said gently. 'I wanted to get the lights on the tree for you . . . before I left.'

'Come upstairs and do it then –'

'No.' Her tenderness was still emphatic. 'You do it . . . don't leave it bare . . .'

Alan sucked in ragged breath, his throat tightening. There had to be something he could say to stop all this, some key word, some clue he'd missed . . .

'Can I drive you anywhere?'

Her 'no' was almost inaudible. She glanced toward the van where her brother-in-law dawdled, gazing conspicuously in every direction but theirs. 'I'll go with George,' she said quickly, then hesitated, the large, dark eyes Alan knew so well fastening on him, soaking up a last, photographic impression. 'Be good,' she added suddenly. And was gone, clattering into the dark as George gestured an apologetic goodbye.

Disbelieving, Alan watched them both squeeze into the cab. The door slammed. The pantechnicon's engine burst into life. Rear lights flashed.

Small, distinct actions Alan saw with absolute clarity, each one marking by heartbeats the inevitability of Maddy's departure. Then it was true, it was really, *really* true . . .

As he had that thought he realized he'd missed the van's first movement. Its metal sides shuddering, it was rolling away into the night, gathering speed, disappearing with remarkable suddenness under the sparse street lighting, round the gentle curve of the road.

Alan stared after it for a long time, daring it to return. But it didn't take up his challenge.

He shivered, suddenly aware that he was in shirtsleeves and sleet was beginning to fall. A light winked at him from a house down the hill. It was a bulb-covered Christmas tree, flashing on and off in an upper window. Emptily, he registered it.

She hadn't even *risked* kissing him goodbye.

2

Monday

An ice-cream war

The digital alarm's gentle thrumming sounded like a midget submarine about to dive. Dragged, groaning, from semi-consciousness, Alan flung out an arm for the snooze button before the machine went into its Simon and Garfunkel selected favourites. It was a double shock to find his fingers flailing empty air. The bedside table had gone and, with it, the bedside lamp. Stretching, he found the alarm on the carpet and managed to avoid all but two bars of *Scarborough Fair*.

He thumped back on to the bare mattress. The leather jacket which covered his lower legs slithered away into the darkness. He felt wretched.

Rest had eluded him as efficiently as sleep. All night long he had ricocheted between outrage and self-recrimination, wild optimism and wilder panic. Now he was simply numbed and gritty behind the eyeballs.

With a supreme effort he rolled back to the edge

of the bed. The alarm's display read four-thirty. Nearly four hours to sunrise. Ninety minutes before he started work.

He showered and dressed listlessly, picking his clothes almost at random from a jumbled heap which had once occupied the well ordered wardrobe, dresser and drawers. At least at this time of the working day he normally functioned on automatic – bedroom to bathroom to bedroom to kitchen to front door – a routine dinned into him by half a decade of unsocial hours. The slow ferment in his brain kept him from noticing much of his surroundings – dimly he was aware that the flat had an unfamiliar, oddly new feel to it, as if he had woken in a strange hotel suite which appeared to contain very little of what it should.

Only when he went to pour breakfast cereal into two bowls (he always left Maddy's breakfast out for her because she didn't get up for work until after eight) did a sharper reality intrude; he only needed *one* bowl today. Or he would have if there had been any.

There weren't any spoons either.

Irritation punctured his numbness. The woman might at least have left him a bowl and a spoon. She *knew* his morning routine. The fact that he was incapable of eating anything, now that he was faced with the prospect, only added to his irritation. Scowling, he went into the hallway, shrugged on his dark overcoat and threw his grey cashmere scarf round his neck. Then he put out all the lights. The pettiness of Maddy's act nagged him all the way down the stairs.

Outside, the night was darker than ever – few

houselights were still visible – but there was a freshness to the air, a sense of the new day stirring into wakefulness just over the hills. Its promise did not match Alan's mood.

Preoccupied, he shambled to the Cabriolet, slotted into its residents' parking spot opposite the main entrance. It was parked close under one of the block's own trendily slim lamp standards, not because the umbrella of light enabled Alan to keep an eye on his prized possession – he couldn't see the spot from his rooftop eyrie – but because thieves might think he could. A night bird cooed distantly as he slipped his key into the lock. Then he saw the grey squiggle of excrement besmirching the reflecting glory of the roof.

Alan's face contorted in horror. Something snapped in him. First the bowl, now this. The whole of nature was taking its cue from Maddy, attacking the last precious vestige of his self-esteem, conspiring to do him down –

Grunting in fury, he yanked out a handkerchief and savaged the offending spot. Almost at once it occurred to him that an observer might regard his ferocity as unwarranted. Self-consciously his eyes wandered to the street and to the dark windows behind him. It was all right. He was quite alone. Frowning anew, he renewed his assault on the Cabriolet's roof. It was several minutes before he stepped back, crouching and moving round the car to examine the gleaming metal from different angles. If any mark remained, only a microscope would detect it.

But as Alan slipped into the driving seat he was still far from satisfied. The mark went deeper than metal. His day hadn't even begun yet and already it felt sullied.

He drove in quickly, gliding through the dark heart of the city in just under ten minutes. Normally it was a journey he stretched to twenty, sometimes longer, relishing the emptiness and silence of streets he might share only with a milk float, a police patrol car, a TIR lorry on an early start.

The quiet time settled his mind, set in motion the slow meshing of professional gears that prepared him for airtime. Today a hundred miles of empty streets could not have quietened his mind.

Metrosound 261 perched on the top floor of a ten-storey office building at the northern tip of the city centre. In the otherwise empty reception a pale woman in a headscarf was uncoiling a hoover.

'Morning, Moira.' Alan spoke automatically.

The woman's face brightened. 'Morning, Dicky!'

The DJs' office smelt of stale tobacco smoke and overheated coffee. There was no one in sight. At this hour only odd engineers and a bleary-eyed sub from the newsroom could be expected. Alan extracted a cup of scalding liquid from the machine, drew his mail from his pigeonhole, his programme box from his locker.

The morning's papers were piled between the typewriters on the central table. He took a selection and pushed them with the mail into his programme box. Then, sipping his coffee, he wandered into the deserted corridor.

The business end of the station had an open-plan layout with soundproof glass screening each of its four pocket handkerchief-sized studios, like so many over-bright aquaria. Steve Kelly, the three to six am man, was in studio four, mouthing noiselessly into his microphone; Peter Lewis, the night newsreader, was sifting hurriedly-typed folios in number one. Both returned waves as Alan passed.

The wall clock in studio three read five ten. Alan closed the heavy door on his inner sanctum and sank into the console chair. It was one of the smallest studios but its position against an outer wall gave superb views across the city. Down there a scattering of lorries crawled southward along the glistening ribbon of the M8. Toy traffic lights rehearsed for the morning rush.

On any other morning the blend of womb-like security and god-like over-view would have reassured him. This morning he barely noticed. For the first time the show was a burden, a necessary chore that distracted him from the proper examination of his misery. But as he pieced it together, the momentum of five years' broadcasting began to operate. Reluctant adrenalin flowed. In a few minutes Maddy had slipped to the back of his skull. She hovered there, murmurous but temporarily subdued, like the onset of a particularly painful headache.

'... and lastly the weather for west central Scotland and the city. This morning will be milder than overnight, but still no sign of a white Christmas ...'

With Peter Lewis on the headphones, Alan kept one eye on the studio console, the other on his young engineer Keith, counting the seconds through the control-room window. The clock read six four. Alan took slow, deep breaths.

'. . . next news at seven. Now stand by for your daily dose of Dicky Bird –'

The news jingle chimed. Keith circled thumb and forefinger. As the jingle died, Alan faded up the live mike.

'Thanks for all that wonderful six o'clock news, Peter. You know, I keep telling him it would be cheaper to telephone the early news to you half a dozen poor souls who've been listening to yawn-a-minute Kelly all night –' he grinned, catching Kelly's two raised fingers from the adjoining studio '–but he won't listen to me –'

He flicked on the jingle machine. Female voices chorused: *'Hello, Dicky, good morning!'*

'Hello!' he responded.

'Hello! Hello!' the girls sang.

'Anyway,' Alan interrupted them, 'the fun starts now because Dicky Bird is here to wake you up and get you to work or home or wherever you plan to be by nine –'

'Don't you know,' the chorus resumed, *'what they say about the early worm?'*

'What do they say?'

'It always gets' – one beat – *'the bird!'*

'Yes –' Alan switched on the turntable. 'It's the Dicky Bird Early Worm Show!'

He whistled a few halting, deliberately off-key notes, fading himself out as a slow Elton John number picked up. He sighed and leaned back, his radio smile freezing.

A knuckle tapped on the door. Steve Kelly's broad, shaggy head filled the glass panel, beaming companionably. He ducked inside. 'Hello there.'

'Hi, Steve –' Alan sniffed and flicked a switch to cue his next record.

'How's it going?'

'Oh, it's okay – okay –' His voice trailed off into listlessness.

Steve frowned. 'You okay, Alan?'

'I'm fine.' Alan tried a thin smile. Kelly's eager-beavery, off-mike as well as on, was legend at the station. It was the very last thing he wanted this morning.

'Keep your pecker up, eh?'

Alan nodded encouragingly as the DJ slipped out.

In the headphones Elton John was on the retreat. Alan touched the mike fader. 'He's done it again, folks. Kelly's fallen asleep at the microphone – I got here just in time.' He winked at Steve's upraised digit through the corridor glass. 'And now – here's a quick traffic round-up. There is absolutely nothing on the streets right now. Not a car in sight. So why don't you take advantage of that. Get in your car and get in to work straightaway. You'll be in three hours early. There'll be another traffic round-up at the same time tomorrow . . .'

He chop-mixed to the second record. It was *Roxanne* by The Police. He grunted at the irony of Friday's choice. But it was all right. He had got over the day's first hurdle. He would be fine, until the show ended.

The city began to hum Dicky Bird's song, its slow heart beating to life along the arteries of motorway and main road. From his window Alan watched the beaded lights of cars cluster and stream, flowing inward with a quickening rhythm: a pulse at six-thirty, another at seven, a third at seven-twenty. Faster and busier, as window lights flickered on in the shops and offices below, and the sky's blackness softened to grey.

The station too started to bustle. Beyond the studio glass the offices filled with journalists and secretaries, engineers and assistants, talking, typing, hustling in a flurry of unheard activity.

Inside, Alan was nearing the climax of the show. 'During that last number, Nancy in the front office came in to tell me that the look-alikes competition has captured your imagination again this week. A man from Paisley just phoned in to say that his wife is the absolute double of Richard Nixon!' He chuckled, catching sight of a slim, darkly attractive young woman slipping into the adjoining studio from the newsroom. She smiled as he lifted a hand.

'Oh, we'll believe anything that happens in Paisley. But the rules are: either a photograph sent up here to the station – or why don't you just pop up and let Nancy check you out in person? And I can tell you that's a journey very well worth making. So there you go now – if you look like anyone outrageously famous, or infamous, same old rules . . . So keep the snaps coming in. And why can't anyone look like Santa, eh? Come on Santas – get your snaps in!'

The studio clock nudged the half hour.

'And here's the lovely Anne to give us the eight-thirty travel round-up. I wonder who Anne thinks she looks like. I think there's a little touch of the Ingrid Bergman's in there . . . How are you, Annie? Are you all right?'

'Thank you, Dicky,' the dark girl laughed, demurely. 'Yes, I'm fine.'

'Okay. Now where should we avoid traffic-wise today?'

'How about everywhere . . .?'

'Oh dear, oh dear, oh dear, I'll leave you to it then . . .' As the traffic report began, Alan pulled off his headphones, picked up the telephone and asked for a line. He dialled quickly.

'Hello, Colin? Yes, it's Alan here. I'm in deep trouble, friend. Can you come over? I'll see you at the flat about eleven, okay? God bless.'

He put the receiver down and slipped the headphones back on. Outside the sky was the colour of dirty pearl. It looked cold and very dull.

The moment his end jingle died Alan felt a curious tide of lassitude sweep over him. If he had considered the effect of emotional trauma, a sleepless night and three hours of enforced jollity he would not have found it so odd.

But he was in no mood to analyse his physical state. Nodding to Keith, he re-filled his programme box and went to deposit it in his locker. The DJs' office still smelled of cigarette smoke and coffee, but it was crowded now. The clatter of typewriters cut through the rumble of conversation. By rights Alan should be typing himself, roughing together the following day's script. At the moment, though, he wanted to do no more than make a brisk exit.

He squeezed past Rufus Dann, the Saturday Show man. An athletic pixy in his tight jeans and red anorak top, the DJ was assaulting a suffering Adler.

'Hi, Rufus –'

'Hey, when you can't slow down and you can't turn around,' the other drawled, 'and you can't trust anyone . . .'

Alan snapped his fingers in recognition. 'Van the man!' He matched Rufus's Caledonian-American: 'You just sit there like a butterfly . . .'

'I'm on my way to see that girl of mine,' Rufus responded. 'Nothin' else matters in this whole wide world . . .'

Alan grunted, feeling a sudden chill at the peculiar irony of the quotation. Rufus's normal method of communication was by rock lyric. Alan hadn't had a sensible conversation with him since 1981.

He slammed his locker door and left.

The front door of the flat thumped shut with a curiously hollow sound that made him pause in suprise. Then he realized. The place was as coldly, echoingly empty as when he had first seen it four years before. Correction. When he and Maddy had first seen it.

Tugging his overcoat collar protectively about

his ears, he moved out of the tiny vestibule into the lounge. Chill winter sunlight flooded through the half-drawn curtains. Its effect was pitiless, picking out neglected scuff marks in the Berber, dust streaks along book shelves denuded of all but Maddy's abandoned romance, a dent in the wallpaper where a frisbee demonstration had gone awry. In the corner, Maddy's Christmas tree hid under an avalanche of gaudy wires and blank bulbs. It looked like an undisciplined extension to the rack system.

Between the speakers slumped an ancient easy chair bequeathed by his mother. There was nothing else in the room. He had forgotten how very big it was.

He crossed to the easy chair and sank slowly into it. Something crackled in his pocket. He pulled out the half a dozen Christmas card envelopes he had picked up in the main entrance. At least she hadn't started re-directing mail yet.

The doorbell rang.

'It's on the latch!'

A heavy tread crushed the tiniest surge of hope. Then a male head popped itself round the door jamb.

'It's only me.'

Alan smiled bleakly.

The head was egg-shaped, eggier than most because the hairline had retreated well over half-way up the dome-like forehead. But the face beneath was youthfully smooth, the eyes crinkly and sharp. They looked as if they might belong to a clever man, a man blessed with a wry humour and a briskly practical view of the world. Fortunately for Alan, they did.

'Maddy Campbell,' he read. 'Maddy Campbell and Alan. Ms Madeleine Campbell. And Alan.' He let the envelopes drop to the carpet, lifting his eyes to his friend. 'She's gone.'

Dr Colin Semple nodded and advanced into the room, his hands deep in his corduroy pockets. He looked round at the empty corners, glanced toward the kitchen-diner. He whistled softly.

'Oh boy – she really meant business, eh?'

'Don't say that –' Alan frowned. He wanted a soothing bedside manner, not statements of the obvious. He had forgotten his old friend's practicality could be as blunt as it was useful.

'What do you want me to say?' Colin replied. 'She'll be back in a day or two with her tail between her legs. And the piano. And the dining table . . .?'

'She left the washing machine. That could be a good sign, eh?'

Colin pursed his lips. 'I don't see Maddy coming back for a washing machine. A fur coat, maybe . . .' He ducked into the bedroom. 'She didn't leave a fur coat, did she?'

Alan shook his head.

Colin turned back, blinking at the scale of the devastation. 'Was *everything* hers?'

'Uh-huh. Except for the mortgage. That was mine. Well, you know Maddy – she was always acquiring things. She *liked* acquiring things.' The sound of himself justifying Maddy suddenly rankled. 'What am I going to do?' he asked.

Colin considered. 'You'll need a table. Definitely a table.'

Alan sighed loudly. Colin felt a pang of self-reproach. He and Alan had known each other from their university days, with Colin cast in the role of elder brother-cum-father confessor, despite being a good six months the younger. It was a role he enjoyed. He tried a more positive approach.

'Do you realize,' he asked, 'how *lucky* you are?'

Alan squeaked incredulously.

'Don't you see what an opportunity you have? How many people our age would give an arm and a leg to be able to break out and start all over again? *A new life!* That's what you've been handed on a plate –'

Alan blinked warily. The plate association was unfortunate since he no longer possessed one on which to be handed anything.

But Colin was pressing on: 'Look around you. Everything here is you. That chair is you.' He faltered, stuck for examples in the room's desolation. 'The book there. It's *you.* There is nothing but you here now – what a chance!'

Alan stirred in grudging acknowledgment of the general idea. It was a little closer to what he'd had in mind.

'You've been submerged in another person's personality . . . you've become a *sub-person.* And now you're free!'

'Thanks a lot,' Alan snorted. 'Why didn't you tell me all this before?'

'Because –' Colin chose his words carefully '– Maddy was utterly fantastic and special, and you deserved as much of her as you were going to get. But now you've had it. It's your turn now.'

Alan grunted and stood up. He shambled towards the window, the struggle to give credence to Colin's view writ large on his face.

His friend watched him closely. Colin had built his medical reputation on his belief in plain-speaking, whenever possible. But it was hardly the moment to point out that Maddy had been a wildly sexy and utterly wilful bitch. Instead he compromised.

'Anyway, there was always something unreal about you two. You were like kids. Playing – and fighting. It was a bit of a caper, wasn't it?'

'No!' It was the word 'unreal' that stung Alan; Maddy had been the most real thing he had ever experienced. 'Don't say that. I worshipped her!'

Colin returned his friend's indignant glance with a wry smile. 'That's not the nicest thing you can do somebody, is it? I hope you don't worship me.'

'No!' The grin surfaced involuntarily. 'You're my friend.'

Colin made no reply. As the implications of his answer worked in his mind, Alan looked away.

A soft bleeping sound, like an electronic asthmatic, arose from Colin's jacket pocket. 'Did Maddy take the telephone?' he asked.

Alan grinned again. 'No –' He nodded at a cable trailing behind a speaker.

Colin followed it and lifted up the telephone. He dialled and asked for an extension. 'It works,' he told Alan wonderingly. 'You're still in business.'

This time Alan's smile was fragile but broad. By whatever strange chemistry, Colin's healing art had started to work its magic again.

Alan listened with gratitude, and more than a hint of envy, as the surgeon rattled off a series of abstruse medical enquiries. Alan had always wanted to do that. Not even a radio celebrity could sound so casually authoritative.

'Good,' Colin concluded. 'You fix up the theatre for two. Get the pre-med finished, and I'll see you in ten minutes. Okay?' He put down the phone. 'Got to go and introduce somebody to a secondhand kidney. What will you do?'

Alan shrugged. He couldn't cap a closing line like that. 'Oh, I'll do some shopping – get some things for the house. Pots, pans . . .' His imagination ran out. None of it seemed very urgent.

'Good lad.' Colin seemed genuinely encouraged. 'Do you want to eat with us tonight?'

'Aye, maybe.' Alan appreciated the offer. 'I'll let you know.'

Colin nodded. He made for the hall.

'Colin!' Alan called suddenly. He hesitated. 'Do you think she loved me?'

His friend paused in the doorway. 'Sure she did,' he said easily. 'She told me one night – when she was drunk.'

Alan swallowed. 'She never told me.'

'Well – she wouldn't.'

Alan digested this, then his brow knitted. 'Where was I while all this was going on?'

'You were through in the kitchen telling Janet you loved *her*. You were drunk too.'

With a wry smile, the surgeon made his exit.

Alan stayed where he was, nodding slowly as memory provoked the ghost of a smile. *That* party . . . Then his frown re-formed itself. Who on earth was Janet?

Colin's medical perspective had shaved the jagged edges off his pain. It hadn't taken it away – he could hardly expect that – but he fancied he saw the first glimmer of hope. *A new life.* The phrase had a brave sound to it. For a non-journalist, Colin had a surprising knack with words.

Alan turned it over in his mind as he parked in Union Street. If he repeated it often enough he might actually believe it. The exercise sustained him during his first foray down Argyle Street.

But as he picked non-expertly among pots and pans, dishes and plates, he was beset by something very different – a curious sense of fragility. He felt like an invalid re-entering the world after a prolonged illness. Someone who smiled too easily, too aware of their vulnerability. A person deserving the sympathy of small dogs and attractive women. Especially the tall blonde ambling down the opposite side of the hardware display to him.

He matched her pace, observing her covertly. She was extremely attractive. High-piled hair like slivers of buttery gold; high, model's cheekbones; narrow, flaring nostrils; eyes, large and thickly lashed, discreetly averted.

She knows, he thought. *She knows I've noticed.*

They reached the end of the display together, turning to face each other. The front wheel of a pram nudged Alan's ankle. With an apologetic cough, he slipped to one side, glimpsing a second infant slung across the blonde's front. She ambled on, blandly ignoring him.

Squashing an embarrassment no one else seemed aware of, Alan moved to the sales counter. As he deposited his selection a tall female figure, long hair ruddily blonde, turned from a wall display. His heart jumped. The woman turned back. Her face was angular, bespectacled; she was well into her forties.

'You know you can have all three pots the same colour?' the sales assistant asked.

He stared at her, still distracted. She was about nineteen, pretty, grinning at him quizzically.

'No. No,' he said, waking up. 'It doesn't matter.'

'Sure?' She seemed happy to oblige him.

'I like the idea of mix 'n match.' He found himself smiling foolishly.

The assistant laughed. She slipped his purchases into a bag. 'Just thought it would look better,' she said, handing it over, her fingers only half accidentally brushing his.

Sweet Jesus, he thought, moving away, *I'm like a babe in arms. Homo domesticus* suddenly adrift on the tides of emotional chance. At the whim of the kind of random romantic urges of his pre-Maddy days. Except he'd quite forgotten how to handle them. He could no more pick up a total stranger than climb Mont Blanc in his training shoes. Or without. The knack had gone, atrophied away through disuse.

His confidence wobbling, he retreated into the street. As he reached the Cabriolet a couple ran, laughing, across the road in front of him. They were in their teens, probably students, the girl tagging in the boy's wake with one hand on a long college scarf wrapped round his neck. They seemed oblivious of anything, anyone beyond their own happiness. The sight applied the *coup de grâce* to his self-confidence. That was the intimacy he really missed. He wouldn't find that in a casual pick-up.

He climbed into the car, his comfortable fragility going bad on him. Suddenly it wasn't winsome or touchingly vulnerable any more. It was cold and empty and shaming. A very private void.

It grew steadily inside him as he drove back to the flat. By the time he had parked outside it was huge. It undermined him at every step, mocking every impulse; it threatened to swallow him whole.

He had only moved a yard or two from the car, his arms laden with packages, when the first hint of panic hit him. He looked up at the windows of the block. Dully the double glazing reflected the physical gloom of approaching dusk. Like rows of dead eyes. He couldn't creep in behind them. Not yet. He wouldn't. He dumped his packages on the back seat of the BMW, jumped in the front and drove.

Thirteen thousand pounds of Teutonic engineering skill throbbing under his rear, Metrosound's Fabulous Forty blaring from the Blaupunkt and the mpg meter screaming extravagance at twenty-two miles to the gallon: *this* was the life. This was the way Dicky Bird handled things. No messing about. Foot down, head up, straight on to the Clydeside Expressway. If plain Alan Bird was a quivering heap of haggis, the Early Worm certainly wasn't. No way.

He shot through the gathering dusk, outpacing his panic, the needle bumping on eighty.

On either side headlamps grew luminous. Up ahead windows began to glow in high rises, stacked like luminous newsprint in the mauve sky.

Unthinkingly he was following a favourite route to work. The Expressway wasn't direct but it gave him the chance to open up the Cabriolet. It also took him straight into the spaghetti tangle of Anderston Cross. And the spotlit glamour of Metrosound's solitary billboard. It reared up now, surreally bright against the dim geometry of fly-overs, the bulk of the Holiday Inn.

'Metrosound 261 – Radio in Three-D!' it announced over three headphoned and grinning heads. 'Dicky Bird, Dave McCree and Rufus Dann!.'

Alan wasn't too sure about the slogan – the brainchild of the station's managing director – but he had no complaints about the picture. Fifty square feet of boyish enthusiasm.

That was a celebrity up there. That was not a man with problems. For a moment, as he braked for the lights, he became his radio self again. At one with the big city. Its favourite son, its representative.

From the door speakers Dave McCree's Highland burr warned of southbound hold-ups, half-mile tailbacks at the Clyde tunnel. As the lights changed, Alan slipped into first, easing forward into the rush-hour throng. He felt an urge to mingle with the commuting masses, to lose himself in the movement of the city.

By the time he had joined the queue to the Kingston Bridge the slow shuffle of the traffic had become hypnotic. Freed from any need to be anywhere apart from where he was, Alan saw the jam in a new light. A battery of lights, in fact. White and red and green and amber. Dark reflections in the tarmac. Grey shimmers in the swirl of exhaust smoke. The traffic moved in its own bizarre rhythm too. A slow inching advance here, a sudden break for freedom there. But all bound together in a mysterious, enforced, shuffling intimacy. Like kids lined up in a school playground, scuffing their heels as the register was called. Bored and restless, smelling their own farts.

Why had he thought of kids?

A large, light-coloured van moved on the passenger side. Alan glanced across at it, catching the words 'Quality Ices' in bright red lettering. His eyes lifted to the selling hatch above it.

And his heart stopped.

For a mad moment he thought he was staring at Maddy. A Maddy perched among wafer packets, confectionery cartons and tubs of raspberry ripple.

She was smiling at him, serenely, knowingly, face framed by the hatch, lit by the flickering kaleidoscope of road lights. Involuntarily Alan smiled back. Maddy's own smile broadened in response, and abruptly the illusion was gone. The girl's face was younger, sharper, her mouth as full but wider, her hair as rich but darker. Yet as she gazed at him, shedding years the longer she looked, her expression still bore tantalizing traces of Maddy. The teasing challenge in her eyes – the tacit awareness of her own beauty. And, *my God,* she *was* beautiful.

Alan's throat dried, his pulses raced. Abruptly the ice-cream van pulled away, sliding into the gloom, the bizarre carriage of a fairy princess, whose retreating smile turned to beckon him on.

In that instant Alan was hooked.

Deliberately, he held back, letting two cars pass in the adjacent lane before indicating left. Two more squeezed through before he could ease into the van's lane.

He began to follow, his eyes fixed on the pale square outline. The van passed under a street lamp. He read across the back 'Mr Bunny (formerly Mr Softy)'. Was that *Miss* Bunny inside? Could that be the ice-cream queen?

At the end of the bridge the van turned east. Alan swung the Cabriolet after it, increasing his distance as the traffic thinned. He felt like the hero of some Forties gangster movie, trailing the heroine, who might also be the villainness, to some illicit rendezvous.

But underneath there was a genuine need to know. Quite what, he wasn't yet sure.

True to its gangster counterpart, the van led him through darker, less familiar streets. Unkempt rows of shops gave way to waste ground and high walls, warehouses and low industrial buildings. It was a part of the city Alan had never visited before. Soon the road snaked across an area of vast desolation. The ghosts of side streets branched off to left and right between the outlines of demolished tenements.

The Cabriolet and the van seemed the only traffic here, and Alan drew back still further, waiting until his quarry had turned a distant corner before squeezing the throttle.

The housing scheme was an abrupt shock. It basked under a sudden profusion of street lamps: an island of concrete and clean brick, gleaming tarmacadam and newly laid paving stone. There was even a hint of grass. The ice-cream van was parked on the first corner. As Alan overtook it its tone hiccupped into life: five rising and falling notes prefaced by a Goofy-voiced 'Hello folks!'

He pulled into the kerb a discreet distance beyond, cut the engine and concentrated on the rear mirror. A queue of half a dozen had already formed at the serving hatch. Too many for the moment.

He had no idea what he was going to do, but he didn't want to share it with an audience.

When only two small children were left, he climbed out of the car, locked the door and strolled casually along the pavement, his hand reaching up to adjust his tie. Only as he felt his open collar did he remember he wasn't wearing one. He drew his scarf up in a tight knot instead.

The van was bathed in the orange glow of an interior light. A compressor murmured soothingly. As Alan drew level with the hatch he saw to his disappointment that the driver was serving. The girl stood toward the front of the vehicle, her back half turned as she unpacked cartons of chocolate bars and sweet packets.

Alan gazed at her, fascinated that her profile

was as entrancing as her full face. She looked almost birdlike in a loose, fluffy, enveloping yellow jumper.

'Yes please, sir?' asked the driver.

Alan's eyes flickered toward the price list.

'Oh – a ninety-nine, please.'

'With or without?'

The driver engaged Alan's full attention for the first time. He was a young man, square-faced and serious in a bomber jacket and tam-o'-shanter.

'Raspberry,' he explained, holding up a plastic bottle.

'Oh – with. Please,' Alan grinned.

She had slim shoulders; Maddy had had slim shoulders. He liked that in a woman.

He became aware that the driver was nudging his knuckles with an ice-cream cornet and frowning. Alan nodded and took it. The girl still hadn't turned.

'And –' he added, suddenly inspired '– a Highland toffee, please.'

Now the girl turned, lifting the sweet from the wall rack. Her fresh, bright, heavy-lashed gaze swept over him. Unsmiling yet not unfriendly. But interested. Definitely interested. Then the driver took the toffee from her and handed it down to Alan, his shoulders filling the hatch. 'There you are,' he said briskly.

Alan thanked him, fumbling in his pockets for the money. He squeezed his change and the toffee bar into his overcoat. A brawny ten-year-old elbowed in front of him with an indignant glare.

Awkwardly, bearing his cornet like a frozen Olympic torch, Alan moved back toward the

Cabriolet. He should have said something. Some bright Dicky Bird-type witticism. She would have heard him and laughed. Perhaps recognized his voice. Started to chat. *That*'s what he should have done.

A large saloon car overtook the ice-cream van and screeched to a halt opposite Alan's BMW. Two men leapt out and sprinted past him.

Instead he had simply gawped like a lovesick fourteen-year-old. The girl must have thought he was . . .

Something odd about the men from the car struck him belatedly. He turned.

The men had just reached the van. They wore dark sweaters with stockings pulled over their heads. There were pick-axe handles and iron bars in their hands. Voicelessly, and with a quite demonic enthusiasm, they began to demolish the ice-cream van.

Alan gaped in shocked disbelief.

The van's windows exploded inwards, sending the driver and the girl cowering beneath the counter. One man started to smash the headlamps. The other belaboured the doors and side panels. As he drew level with a shattered window the driver jumped up inside and began hurling white dollops of ice-cream with a scoop.

Heavily spattered, the attackers transferred their attention to the rear tyres. Instantly the rear door burst open and the driver and the girl charged out, yelling and brandishing bottles of raspberry essence. They began to squirt their assailants, drenching them in bright sticky fluid.

'Bastards . . . bastards . . .' hung on the still air.

Beaten back, the masked men aimed last blows at the van's side panels, then retreated at speed.

With a jolt, Alan realized they were coming straight for him. An involuntary squeak popped out of his throat. He turned and bolted. Ahead of him the attackers' car was moving slowly up the road, its doors open, engine revving. To his horror Alan found the masked men drawing level with him.

It had only just begun to dawn on him that they were a lot keener on making their escape than bothering him when the nearest suddenly blinked at him and slowed. Speechless, Alan slowed too, backing away before the man's inquisitive advance until he felt the roof of the Cabriolet dig into his back.

'Hey!' the man cried excitedly. 'It's you, isn't it? It's Dicky Bird!' Ice-cream and raspberry essence daubed his head like the markings of some bizarre Glaswegian totem pole.

Wide-eyed, Alan stared at the iron bar in the other's fist.

The man turned and bawled at his companion. 'Dicky Bird's here!'

'Come on to hell!' the second attacker yelled. He was halfway into the car. 'Let's get out of here!'

Instantly Alan felt himself gripped and shaken, his cornet flying from his fingers.

'Gi'us an autograph, Dicky!'

The violence released Alan's tongue. 'I don't have a pen on me –'

'Get in the car for God's sake!' the second attacker screamed.

A frown creased what little Alan could see of the first man's face. He tossed his head angrily in the second attacker's direction, then he turned back, his eyes widening with a sudden inspiration. 'Give us a dedication at least, Dicky, eh?' He retreated, gesturing with his iron bar. 'For my mother . . . tomorrow morning? Have you any Mantovani or Dean Martin?'

Alan was nodding furiously. 'Bound to, bound to . . . What about *Memories are made of this*?'

'Aye, lovely!'

The raider was at the car door, grinning happily. He gave a last wave with his iron bar, then, as though finally realizing the violent implications of this, laughed and made a thumbs-up sign instead. He was still doing it when his companion dragged him inside. The door slammed. With a squeal of tyres the car roared off into the night.

Alan breathed out slowly. His hands were trembling. His heart fluttered in his chest like a trapped bird. Where in God's name was he? Chicago? This was Glasgow, not the Wild West.

He breathed in again, more easily, blinking as he lifted his head. Glass tinkled distantly in the van.

The van – the girl!

He must have been dreaming or stunned. He ran.

Both driver and girl were inside as he reached the wrecked vehicle. They were working feverishly, piling debris, brushing out broken glass.

'Can I help you, sir?' the driver gabbled through the hatch. 'A refill for your ninety-nine?'

'Are you okay?' Alan gasped.

'Oh yes, yes – everything's under control – don't worry about a thing – is there something you wanted?'

Alan frowned. The man was hardly looking at him. Scarlet liquid dripped from his brow.

'Are you hurt?' Alan persisted. 'Is that blood?'

'Eh!' Alarm flashed across the driver's face. He felt his forehead. 'Oh no, no . . . that's just raspberry essence – don't worry about a thing – just some high-spirited youths, that's all – now if there's nothing else you want I think we better be going –' Abruptly he turned back into the van.

Alan stared after him, confused, unnerved by the man's extraordinary behaviour. Surely this sort of thing wasn't normal around here? The van's engine coughed into life. With a grating sound, the vehicle lurched forward, crunching through broken glass, shattered cornets and spattered ice-cream. Alan watched it negotiate a painful half circle and move off, wheezing gently, the way it had come. As the darkness swallowed it up its tone gave a last hiccup: a slurred 'Hello f–' followed by a strangled squeak. Then it had gone.

Alan shook his head, turning in dazed wonderment to the empty street. Not a soul had appeared. Not even a curtain had so much as twitched. And there could have been bloody murder here only seconds ago!

He made a tiny, shrugging, impotent gesture with his shoulders and was suddenly aware that his limbs were still shaky. That was the effect of the violence. Sudden, unprovoked, *insane* violence. It was incredible.

He plodded back toward the Cabriolet, glancing behind him again and again as if to reassure himself it had really happened. But for the congealing mess in the road he might have hallucinated everything. That, and something else.

His ninety-nine cone stood up like a clown's hat on the metal rim of the BMW's canopy, the ice-cream a near perfect three-inch circle beneath it. It was the exact spot besmirched by the bird that morning.

The shot of whisky bit hard at the back of Alan's throat, almost as hard as the foam-covered wooden slats in his mother's bequeathed easy chair. He gulped and winced at the taste. He didn't like whisky much. It was only kept in the flat because Maddy liked it; he had been surprised to find any left. But he needed a stiff drink. Badly.

Maddy – deceptive blonde mums in hardware departments – flirting shop assistants – sloe-eyed ice-cream princesses – and now an ice-cream war! It had been twenty-four hours of sex and violence. It was all very well taking Colin's advice and living a new life, but on current evidence this particular new life was living him. He took another swallow, feeling the rosy effects of the first begin to mellow his tired brain.

What on earth *had* he witnessed this evening? Those men weren't high-spirited youths – they were fully-grown thugs. But who got that upset about ice-cream, for heaven's sake? It had been the van they had been attacking, not its occupants. A single blow from that iron bar would have flattened the driver and the girl. He shuddered at the memory of its proximity. *Gi'us an autograph, Dicky* . . . Jesus. He snorted derisively.

Perhaps he should have reported it. That hadn't occurred to him till now. Mr Bunny – if that's who it was – had been so *dismissive* of the entire incident. *He* didn't want to report anything. And no one had actually been hurt. How did the law stand on a severe bout of raspberry essence daubing?

His brain rebelled. It was late. He'd already missed a night's sleep. Alan Bird needed his rest if Dicky was going to sparkle in the wee small hours. He would go to bed and try to dream of fairy princesses offering him lasciviously shaped ninety-nines. But not of Maddy. Definitely not of Maddy.

Drowsiness blurred any memory of lurching to the bedroom. He was surprised to find a brand-new set of pyjamas, still cellophane-wrapped, on the end of the bed. Dimly he remembered some long-lost gift from a relative; they must have been unearthed from the bottom of a departed drawer. He tore off the wrapping, grimacing at the red-striped winceyette. Grandpa's jammies. The final death of romance. He hadn't worn pyjamas for four years. But they would keep him warmer than last night under his overcoat and his leather jacket and his scattering of old pullovers.

He was asleep before he had even covered himself.

The ringing came from a great distance and

sounded odd, as though the miniature submarine inside his digital alarm had finally submerged. After long, sleep-fugged moments trying to make the sound fit, he realized it was the front doorbell. Only half-conscious, he stumbled from the bed, found the light switch and fumbled his way into the hall. His eyes were still slitted against the brightness as he cracked open the door.

Maddy stood on the doorstep. She was smiling, her face nestled in the collar of her fur coat, her high cheekbones flushed with cold.

'Maddy!'

Joy rocketed within him. Instantly she was clinging to him, covering his face and neck in kisses. Helpless, gasping in happy shock, he was driven back along the hallway.

'Have you still got a bed?' she whispered.

'Oh Maddy – I've missed you – I've wanted to talk to you –' The words burst out in a gabble.

She silenced him with a finger to his lips. 'We can talk in the morning.'

'Okay. Okay.' He'd agree to anything. He'd stand on his head. He'd swim the Atlantic. 'Oh, Maddy –!'

They tumbled on to the mattress, Maddy on top. 'Where did you get the pyjamas?' She plucked, frowning, at his sleeve.

'Aunt Polly sent them – I won't need them any more – oh –' He began kissing her chin, drinking in her perfume.

She lifted her head, looking down at him.

'Can I stay the night?'

'You can stay forever, Maddy,' he sighed. 'You know that.'

'Okay.' She cocked her head in the way he loved, letting her thick hair sweep across her cheek. 'I'll stay for ever.'

'Oh, Maddy –' he laughed, grasping her to him. 'Oh Maddy, Maddy, Maddy –'

She felt wet. *Wet*? Was it snowing outside?

As he shifted to feel more of her, the mattress grew rigid and hard beneath him, gouging his back and thigh muscles. With a grunt of discomfort he sat up. His whisky tumbler rolled off his knees, where it had spilled, and thumped on to the living-room carpet.

He was alone, quite alone, with a hammering, joyous heart, his dreams and whisky-wet trousers. The disappointment welled in him with a taste like bile.

For a moment the disparity between his dream self and his real self was so appalling he was unable to believe it. Then after a few more minutes he did.

He dragged himself out of the easy chair, padded blindly into the bedroom and collapsed across the bed. The last thing he remembered was a shirt button that stubbornly refused to undo.

3

Tuesday

Angry seas

Alan was feeling slightly better than average when he slipped out of the block the following morning, given that his current average was a shade off suicidal. He had slept leadenly but well. He had even found a tie to wear.

Then he pushed the key into the Cabriolet's lock, squeezed the door handle and frowned. It wouldn't budge. Which meant that he must have left it unlocked. He never did that.

Something white caught his eye through the amber reflection of the overhead lamps. He turned the key again and whipped open the door.

'Oh shit –'

Blinking on, the interior light disclosed over two dozen ice-cream cones upended evenly across the front seats.

Incoherent curses bubbled through Alan's lips. He began lifting out the nearest cones, dashing them disgustedly into the road. He reached an old newspaper from the back and tried to scrape congealed ice-cream off the velour. White blobs fell on the carpeting.

Then he saw the piece of card propped against the gear change. He bent and picked it up. Neat, biro-written capitals announced:

> DICKY,
> SILENCE IS GOLDEN.
> WILL ALSO BE GOOD FOR YOUR CAR.

It all made perfect sense. Of course ice-cream vans weren't routinely demolished on the city's housing estates. He had blundered into something as deadly serious as it was bizarre. But why, oh why, did they have to attack his car?

'. . . Yes, memories certainly used to be made of that. Nice to hear from the old crooner again. I wonder is the Rat Pack still running? Probably on crutches by now. But enough idle speculation for one day. That's all from your old Early Worm, Dicky Bird, until some God-awful time tomorrow morning. You'll be there . . . I hope I'll be – or is it the other way around? Anyway, stand by for the national news on the hour!'

Alan keyed up his end music, counted two beats and continued: 'Stay tuned to the only station in town. This is Dicky Bird saying cheerio. And I hope something nice – something awfully nice – happens to you today. Cheery-bye!' Another burst of music. 'Don't count on it!'

He let the music ride, started a slow fade and cut it as a commercial took over. He sniffed and peeled off his headphones and his Early Worm mask in a single swift movement. All in all, considering the time he'd spent on preparation, the show hadn't gone too badly. He reached across the console and thumbed the intercom button.

'Keith!'

The engineer lifted his head on the other side of the control-room glass. 'Yeah?' His spindly frame was draped with his jet black 'I wish I was deep instead of just macho' tee-shirt.

'Fix me up a booth for ten o'clock, will you? I'd like to do some trails and some commercials for the weekend. You could edit them, okay?'

'Sure thing, Alan.'

Another thought struck Alan. Engineers were supposed to be practical people. He thumbed the button again.

'Keith – what would you use to clean ice-cream stains off velour upholstery?'

'Has the ice-cream dried?'

'I'm afraid so.'

Keith grunted sagely. In view of the fact that he was fourteen years Alan's junior he did it very well. 'That sounds like a hot water and detergent job – but you'd have to wet the whole seat so it wouldn't leave a mark. It'll be tricky . . .'

Alan nodded. He'd thought so. Being practical generally was. Then he saw Keith grinning.

'Here, are you sure it's ice-cream?'

'Cheeky monkey.' Alan cut the intercom.

Voice-overs provided the icing on Alan's cake. Dicky Bird might keep the mortgage paid and the larder full, but advertising blurb made Cabriolets possible. The only drawback to this near perfect arrangement was that from time to time he actually had to sit down and do the things.

The recording booth Alan used was fractionally larger than a telephone kiosk. There was just enough room for a chair, a shelf and a microphone. Alan ran a poor fourth.

He sat in headphones, watching Keith through a glass panel opening on to an only marginally more spacious control room. Both beat time to a jingle. At the right moment Keith aimed a warning finger. But Alan was already poised at the mike.

'Thrifty Pops! Thrifty Pops! You just munch them all day! They never stop!'

He grimaced as the jingle filled in again, deeply thankful he only had to *sound* enthusiastic. Over a backing track of feverishly smacking lips, he finished: 'Thrifty Pops – the big, *big* bag of munchies that lasts *all* day . . .' When the lips stopped smacking he looked up at Keith. 'How was that?'

The engineer seemed unimpressed. 'Well, it was a bit dry, maybe –'

'You ought to try Thrifty Pops,' murmured Alan, who had. 'Okay, keep that one. We'll try one more.'

The jingle squealed and jibbered in reverse. It began to replay. Alan nodded in time with the music. 'Thrifty Pops! Thrifty Pops!' he began. 'You just eat them all day! They never –'

'No, no, no –' Keith cried, killing the sound. 'You said "eat", Alan. It should be "munch".'

'Oh, shit –!'

Alan sighed, then took a deep breath as the tape rewound. He wasn't concentrating, and if he didn't concentrate he wouldn't please Louis, the advertising manager. If he didn't please Louis that would be another Cabriolet repayment he wouldn't make. God, didn't he have enough on his newly-purchased plate with Maddy and ice-cream maniacs assaulting his peace of mind? But halfway through the next take it was he who called for a halt.

'No, no – there's something wrong – the rhythm's wrong. It's the "you". It doesn't need the "you" – who wrote this stuff? There's no rhythm in it. Spin it back . . .'

Keith shrugged compliantly. He was used to tantrums at this game.

Bracing himself, Alan tried his revised version.

'Thrifty Pops! Thrifty Pops! Just munch them all day! They never stop!'

He indicated to Keith to go on to the finish. Then, as the lip smacking died, he beamed encouragingly.

Keith failed to pick up his cue. 'Well, I'm not so sure,' he said. 'I think the "you" had something. It broke the beat . . . the way it came in on the sub-beat was quite special . . .'

'Okay! Okay –' Alan was getting very tired of all this. 'We'll do it again.'

They re-ran the original version.

'Right!' Alan finished. 'Give Louis takes one and four complete and the end part of take three. If he doesn't like that tell him he can get Orson Welles next time.'

'Get you –' Keith commented with a mock

moue, though quietly because Alan was still fourteen years his senior. But the other had already gone.

Thrifty Pops! If the things didn't taste like desiccated cardboard he might have felt better about it. But not much.

He had started in this game as a journalist, not as a media clown. Even Dicky Bird was pushing it. He brought people together, got the day underway with a smile. But smiles weren't much use when there were gangsters roaming the streets, wrecking innocent ice-cream vans, and even more blameless BMW 323i Cabriolets.

Simmering outrage sharpened instincts Alan had not used since his local paper days. Something had to be done. Something journalistic. Something appropriate to his new life.

His heartbeat quickened at the thought. It was the first time his enthusiasm had been engaged – really engaged – for longer than he remembered. Perhaps Colin had been right. Perhaps he had been a *sub-person.* Either way it was a good sign. Too good to sit on. He postponed an immediate plan to work on tomorrow's Early Worm script and went to request an audience with the station's managing director.

'I'll find out if he's free,' said Nancy in reception. She was a small blonde girl, plumply attractive in a white dress which curtained her bosom in Victorian-style lace. Alan's gaze drifted to it idly as she dialled a number on the internal telephone. His fingers tapped out the rhythm of a song he hummed. To his horror he recognized it suddenly as the Thrifty Pops jingle.

'Two minutes' time,' Nancy was saying. 'Thanks, Gloria.'

Alan nodded as she put down the phone. 'Lovely. How's the look-alikes competition coming along, by the way?'

'Fine. Everybody still wants to look like Princess You-know-who, though.'

Alan gave the counter a last tap. 'I'm going to get my dentist to write in. He's the absolute spitting image of George C. Scott.'

Leaving Nancy to digest the significance of this, he scurried away down the abbreviated corridor that housed the administrative department. He passed Rufus, slinking in the opposite direction.

'I hear the seven deadly sins and the terrible twins came to call on you . . .' the latter intoned.

Alan snapped his fingers. 'Dire Straits!'

'The bigger they are, babe, the harder they fall on you . . .'

Rufus's drawl faded round the corner.

Shaking his head, Alan knocked on the door marked 'Managing Director' and went inside.

The secretary's office was empty, the door to the MD's office beyond slightly ajar.

'Hell-o!' he called. He shut the door behind him, cancelling the chatter of typewriters, and immediately heard a soft giggle from the further room.

'Stop your nonsense, Gloria,' came Hilary Sandeman's rumbling burr.

'No, that's not fair,' a female voice bleated.

'It's absolutely fair! I'm allowed to do that –'

There was an explosion of laughter. Smiling, Alan padded across the office and hovered at the crack in the door.

'Hold it! Hold it! I can't get in if you put your finger there,' Hilary complained.

'You'll have to be quicker than that,' said his secretary, who then squealed with mirth. 'You did that while I wasn't looking!'

Curiosity overcame Alan's reserve. He nudged open the door and ducked his head inside.

Hilary Sandeman, managing director and major shareholder of Metrosound 261, was hunched over a business computer's VDU, down whose phospher green surface space invaders resolutely marched. His secretary hunched at his side. Alan's presence registered belatedly.

'Yes, well, I think that'll be all, Gloria – for the moment,' Hilary said with sudden briskness, rising and snapping off the display.

With a residual giggle, Gloria left, easing past Alan with a smile. She was small and blonde with a markedly larger bosom than Nancy's.

Hilary's taste in female employees was as well known and as smilingly remarked upon among station staff as his over-genial and disarmingly false paternalism – a trait learned through long years on the boards as the speaking half of the accordion-playing Sandeman Boys. It was an act that still aroused fond memories in the hearts of the Sandeman clan, but in few other places.

Long hours, low earnings and one particularly distressing evening at the Glasgow Empire had led to Hilary's early retirement, and the concentration of his devious talents on the business side of show business. He had prospered, and nowhere more spectacularly than in local radio. But his memories of grease-paint were strong and he felt the need to compensate himself for its loss – and to boost his newfound respectability – by dressing with ostentatious expense, including the half pound or so of gold jewellery which jingled at his wrist as he beckoned Alan to a chair.

'That phone-in joke spot on Monday was ace, Alan. Tip-top,' Hilary beamed, settling behind his desk. 'I hope you'll keep it in.'

Alan thanked him. Hilary's praise was invariably lavish – it didn't, after all, cost him any money. But it was still pleasant to receive.

'Now,' said Hilary, 'what can I do for you?'

Alan made a small shrugging gesture with his hands. 'I just wanted to talk. I think things are changing. I think *I'm* changing – maybe . . .'

Hilary's genial expression clouded. 'I don't think it's a good time to talk about money, Alan. The Christmas bonus is in the pipeline – you know that –'

'Oh no, it's not money, Hilary,' Alan interrupted. 'I don't mean money, I mean formats . . . programmes . . . other things that maybe I could handle.'

Rain threatened in Hilary's clouds. In his experience a disavowal of interest in cash meant quite the opposite. 'What do you mean?'

'I'm not a kid,' said Alan. 'I'm a serious person. I've got serious friends. Maybe I should be more – serious – sometimes. On the air –'

Now Hilary looked simply worried. 'I don't

catch your drift . . .'

Alan made a big effort. 'I'm not just a *clown*. Maybe I could do other kinds of shows . . . like a documentary . . .'

'Documentary?' Comprehension finally drained from Hilary's face.

'It's a *real* kind of show,' Alan explained with all the enthusiasm of someone who has only just thought of something. 'It's got real things in it . . . people . . . things that happen in the streets. I could follow something up, and make a show. In depth,' he added for effect.

Hilary nodded, relaxing. He had suddenly realized what must be causing this confusion. 'Rufus told me about Madeleine leaving,' he said.

'Who the hell told Rufus?' Alan snapped. 'Anyway, it's got nothing to do with Maddy. This is work. I think I'm on to something – I want to chase it up – make a programme. You know, there are things going on in this town that would make your hair curl –'

Hilary smiled. He knew that. He'd been at the Glasgow Empire in 1954.

He climbed to his feet and moved to the window, gazing out. Then he rocked back on his heels, throwing a warm glance over his shoulder. Alan took his cue and joined him. He had seen Hilary in this mood before.

'Have I ever told you about my Navy days?' Alan didn't bother to reply; it was not required. 'We used to do ship-to-ship transfers – you know, by breeches-buoy. Just a little bucket seat way out on the ocean. Well, there was a point when you were halfway between one ship and the other, and the swell would sometimes put both ships out of sight. Maybe for fifteen, twenty seconds. And there you'd be – hanging below a bit of rope – nothing all around you but angry water . . .'

He glanced meaningfully at Alan who had often wondered why Hilary kept a photograph of a young man in able seaman's uniform at the corner of his desk. He had assumed obscurely that it was there to add class.

'Do you get my point?' Hilary smiled.

Alan glanced at him. He had been waiting for the end of the story. 'Not exactly,' he said.

Hilary frowned. 'You're sure you don't get the point?'

Alan looked blank.

'It's depression, Alan! Depression. You're stuck between where you've been and where you're going, and you've lost sight of both. The way ahead is – faith. Next time you look up the way ahead will be clear. Think about it . . .'

Alan thought about it.

'Can I make a documentary anyway?'

Hilary turned to drape a benign arm over Alan's shoulder. His own wisdom affected him very deeply. 'Alan, the resources of the station are yours to make use of – you know that. But I don't see any need to tamper with the Dicky Bird Early Worm Show, do you?'

'Fair enough,' Alan agreed, satisfied. 'I can pick up a tape recorder from the news room?'

'Of course you can.'

Hilary retrieved his arm as Alan made for the door. 'Knock on my door any time, Alan,' the managing director added. 'And don't fret about these angry seas below you . . .'

'I'll be seeing you, Hilary.'

The door closed behind him. Hilary stood thoughtfully a moment, then picked up the internal telephone.

'Gloria? Get on to the legal department, will you? I want the lowdown on Alan Bird's contract. See if it's yearly or six-monthly. And find out if there's a sanity clause. What?' His face twisted in disbelief. 'No, *sanity* clause.'

He put down the telephone, shaking his head. 'Santa Clause . . .' he sighed. Sometimes blonde hair and big bosoms weren't quite enough.

One hundred years ago ships had flocked to this grey stretch of water, their masts and rigging clustered like a leafless forest, their smoke stacks coughing grime into the noisy air. Today nothing of that remained. A twentieth-century broom had swept by, gathering up dirt and ships and wharves, leaving the clear, chill air of the Clyde to waft freezingly under the single span of the Kingston motorway bridge.

Alan paused at the quayside. Stunted grass grew between the cobbles at his feet. A wind-stripped sapling rattled in the breeze. The peeling doors of the warehouse at his back were locked and bolted and rusted shut.

Living history. That's what this scene was. A perfect image for the changing heart of the city.

Alan was glad he had chosen it for his opening. He was rather less enthralled with the weight of the so-called portable recorder that hung on a strap from his neck. He had been of the opinion that news reporters used lightweight, palm-sized cassette jobs these days. Which only showed him what little interest he had taken in news.

Not any more. He cleared his throat, lifted the hand mike and turned the machine on.

'Dicky Bird. Documentary. Bird's Eye View. Take one,' he announced, watching the sound-level dials flicker.

That didn't sound right. He stopped the machine and re-started it.

'*Alan* Bird. Documentary. Bird's Eye View. Take one.'

That suited his new seriousness more. This time he left the recorder running. He cleared his throat.

'Here I am in the heart of the city, talking to you about . . . this place . . .'

He paused, then snapped off the machine. That didn't sound right, either. It needed more shape, more emotion. He tried again.

'We all think we know our own place – our own town. But do we? How much *do* we know? Or care? Things happen around us . . .' His voice trailed off. He was bumbling. He wasn't *moving* anywhere. Go back to the beginning. What had set this whole business off?

'The other night,' he spoke briskly, 'I saw two men demolish an ice-cream van with iron bars – can you believe it? Right here in this city . . . There are things going on that would –'

He swore under his breath and stopped a third time. Irritation pricked him. He was Dicky Bird, for heaven's sake, the original top-of-the-head man. But the words – the thoughts he knew he had – just wouldn't come together.

He paced down the quay, forgetting the burden of the recorder, treading out his frustration. Perhaps he was only fitted for the Early Worm Show after all.

No. Think. *Think.*

He sank on to a rusted iron bollard, pulling his overcoat collar tight as wind ruffled the water below him. But as he lifted the mike again, only one thought rang through his head with undiminished clarity.

'Maddy . . . please come home. I want to see you today. I want to see what you're wearing. I want you to tell me a joke. I want to make you something nice to eat . . .'

In this empty place the tape reels spun on soundlessly.

He wouldn't despair. Not of the Maddy situation. Not of the ice-cream BMW blackmailers either. He refused to. There was a pattern there. He knew it. Something connected these events. Some underlying reality. If he could just tease it into the open . . .

He sellotaped the large sheet of white paper to the bare wall next to his stereo rack and leaned back on the carpet to study it. The words ICE-CREAM were pencilled in sprawling capitals across the middle. Around them in a straggling circle were grouped six more: HAMMER, RASPBERRY, GIRL, MAN, MASK, CITY. Arrows indicated obscure correspondences.

Visual representation. Flow charts. *Picture* the

problem. This was the new approach he needed.

He sipped at Maddy's whisky, noting with mild surprise that he was beginning to develop a taste for it.

Any minute now meaning would float to the surface, flash between the arrows of his chart. He sensed it. He decided to help it along with another try on the tape recorder. Provide an aural focus.

He pulled the machine closer along the living-room floor and turned it on. He picked up the microphone.

'Ice-cream is not something many of us give a great deal of thought to. Especially at this time of year – with the weather getting that wee bit colder . . .'

He found his eyes glazing momentarily. Words didn't focus his thoughts; they simply jumbled them again. Why on earth had he put an arrow between 'Raspberry' and 'City'? What possible connection did Glasgow have with sticky red fruit essence? The chart didn't clarify things at all. It made them even more confused.

The spectre of Maddy, of the void that still underpinned everything loomed threateningly in his consciousness. He struggled on, faltering: 'It's a kiddy's kind . . . of . . . a . . . thing . . .' But his free hand was already grasping the telephone, lifting the receiver, dialling.

'Hello, Colin?' he interrupted himself. 'Yes, it's Alan . . . This is an SOS. Can I come over?'

The flames crackled from an iron hearth that had once warmed wealthy Glasgow coal merchants.

Its heat billowed upward to the high, Victorian ceiling, buffeted Alan's knees as he slumped in his modern, black leather armchair. There was something solid about this room, Alan decided. Something reassuringly established, that somehow included all the stripped pine, the TV and video in the corner and the brightly coloured children's playthings peeping from behind the sofa.

It was a direction, he realized, in which he had pictured Maddy and himself heading one day. Not in the immediate future, perhaps. But in a year or two.

He cut off the thought, reproving himself, and found Colin's eyes watching him quietly over his whisky glass.

Alan grunted an apology for his brooding silence. He was hardly acting the part of the companionable guest. 'How was the operation yesterday?' he asked.

Colin looked puzzled. He had been in the theatre on and off until late evening. Then he made the connection.

'Oh, yeah – that was fine. The bugger had eaten a sandwich the night before and not told us. I very nearly sewed his new kidney on to a piece of tomato.' Alan chuckled. 'The one essential is a good empty gut,' Colin went on. 'But the kidney seems like a good match.' He sipped at his drink. 'What did *you* do last night?'

He spoke as if the question were loaded, which to him it was. To his surprise Alan answered quite positively: 'Oh, I bought some ice-cream.'

Colin waited for more, but that was all. Evidently there was a meaning here which had escaped him. 'Oh –' he said, non-committally.

Alan nodded. 'Do you know anything about ice-cream?' he asked, sitting up. 'I mean, professionally? Medically? Chemically . . .?'

This didn't help at all. Colin shook his head. 'Not a lot, no –' An outburst of childish wailing from the adjoining hall interrupted him. 'You should ask the experts,' he suggested as the door swung open.

As Alan laughed a blonde, button-eyed, two-year-old girl sidled in, clasping a battered teddy and its detached left arm to her crisp white blouse. Shyly she squirmed on to Colin's lap, pressing the casualty into his hands. 'Daddy fix,' she murmured.

'I've left my needle and thread at the hospital, sweetheart,' Colin warned. He juggled the bear to get a better look at it. 'Oh, this is a mess, Sarah. I've told you not to rush into amputations. You just watch them closely and only chop if you have to . . .'

Clearly Colin's humour did not carry through to the young. The little girl burst into a fresh flood of tears.

'I wish I could cry like that,' Alan commented ruefully. 'I've forgotten how to.'

Colin nodded at the glass Alan held. 'Have another couple of those and it'll all come back.' As Alan smiled Colin pulled his daughter's head against his shoulder. The tears continued. 'That's serious medical advice,' he went on. 'Sometimes there's nothing like a good skinful.'

The hall door opened again and Colin's wife Fiona bustled in, trailing a demure six-year-old edition of herself. Both were small and slim with thick black hair.

'Stay the night, Alan,' the original version offered, scooping up a still tearful Sarah. 'The girls can double up.'

'Do you want me to come up with them?' Colin asked quietly.

His wife shook her head, comforting the little blonde girl. Her sister leaned one-leggedly against Colin's armchair, stretching up to whisper in his ear. As she finished she gazed, bright-eyed, at a bemused Alan. It had been a long time since he had witnessed such domestic intimacy.

'Lily says you can get her ready for bed tonight, Uncle Dicky,' Colin announced importantly. 'Now that's a great honour . . .'

Alan cocked an appreciative eyebrow, uncertain how to respond. Lily was still gazing at him fixedly.

'Girls in the bunk – Dicky in the bed – all right?' declared Fiona, clutching her elder daughter's hand.

'Yes,' Lily whispered.

'Night, night, ladies,' Colin said.

'Kiss daddy goodnight,' Fiona prompted. Lily planted an awkward kiss on her father's cheek. He reached up to ruffle Sarah's blonde head, still buried in Fiona's bosom. 'Goodnight, sweetheart.' The familial entourage departed, the sound of tears retreating up the staircase.

Alan sat back in the sudden silence. 'You lucky bugger,' he said with unabashed envy. 'How did you get it all together? You're so – productive . . .'

'*Re*productive,' Colin corrected. 'There's a difference. Don't forget,' he added, 'I was always jealous of you at university. Organizing the hops – Mr Showbiz – pulling girls . . .'

'Failing exams . . .'

Colin nodded quickly. 'Yeah – even that made me jealous. I didn't have the guts to fail exams –'

Alan grunted, acknowledging his friend's efforts. 'You're just trying to make me feel better.'

'Well, that's my job.' Colin grinned. He watched Alan take a sip of his drink. 'I only hung around you because you knew all the fast girls.'

'Yeah –' Alan lowered his glass. 'But you got one to keep – you married one of them. I don't even have a home . . . You drive round this city and all you see are homes . . . and I don't have one.'

The void showed in Alan's face, alarming his friend. This was a stage beyond the numbness he had displayed already, and not a good sign. Colin resorted to humour.

'We all have worries, you know. I have this recurring nightmare about you coming to date one of my daughters in about ten years' time. It's awful!'

To his relief the blankness went.

'Well,' Alan replied in the measured tones of a joint patter that went back to their early twenties, 'they *will* be old enough to know their own minds, Colin . . .'

'Well, imagine –' Colin responded, warming to his theme. 'That little madam wanting you to undress her tonight . . . six years old!'

They both chuckled brightly, companionship restored, though it was Alan who paused first to drain his glass. He still saw the little girl's grey-green eyes gazing at him with a disturbing directness. Was it just his warped imagination or were there really traces of Maddy, and the ice-cream princess, in that level stare?

It was after midnight when he eased open the door to the girls' bedroom and slipped inside, allowing the light from the landing to guide him to the low bed against the wall. The girls were bundled shapes in the bunks on the opposite side of the room. Only Sarah's blonde tresses, turned silvery in the dim light, differentiated them.

Alan's trousers gave him the most trouble. Generous quantities of Colin's liquor had not improved his sense of balance. Finally he lurched sideways on to the end of the bed. There was a loud squeak which made him wince. He righted himself slowly, but when he kicked off his trousers the squeak came again. He swore silently, fumbled under the duvet and pulled out a large rubber frog.

Depositing it on the floor, he crawled up the narrow mattress, dragging the small pink and gold duvet over his back. As he dropped his head thankfully on the pillow the loudest squeak of all burst in his ear. There was another frog, its quivering green legs projecting from the pillow slip.

'Night, night, Dicky,' came a soft whisper from across the room. Alan looked up from pushing the second frog under the bed. A pale face showed in the upper bunk.

'Night, night, Lily,' he hissed.

'Will you be staying tomorrow night?'

'I don't think so.'

The pale face nodded. 'Will you play me a record?'

'On the Saturday show. I promise –'

'It's for Andrew. Don't mention my name.'

Alan shook his head resolutely.

'Night, night, Dicky.'

'Night, night.'

The whispering subsided.

When Alan crept out of the house just after four the following morning he was careful to squeeze the heavy latch shut on the big, brass-knockered front door. But the sharp click of the mechanism sounded oddly muted anyway. Then he turned and saw the snow. Under the light from the street lamp guarding the curving drive, it was a grey blanket, masking the low hedge, the lawn, the gravel, and the bonnet and canopy of the Cabriolet.

Shivering in the damp cold, Alan stamped over to the car, pleased with the way the soft flakes flew up from his brogues. Snow always aroused a childish delight in him.

He swept a light covering off the windscreen. And started. A pale, triangular face blinked up at him through the perspex. A face framed by tousled strands of strawberry blonde.

He snatched open the driver's door, gaped inside. Maddy frowned up at him, half sprawled across the front seats under the thick layers of newspaper he had used to cover the ice-cream damage. She looked as if she had been asleep.

'What happened to the car?' she asked, blearily.

'Ice-cream cones,' Alan stuttered. Something strange was happening to his heart. He didn't seem able to breathe.

Maddy squirmed upright in the passenger seat. She shuddered, pulling her fur coat tight around her. 'Take me home,' she wailed. 'I'm freezing –'

Disbelieving, Alan squeezed in beside her. Her arm came across his chest. She nuzzled into him. He found his breath at last. 'How did you find me?'

'I tried you at home.' She shook hair out of her eyes. 'The rest was easy.'

Alan swallowed hard. He didn't want to touch her in case she wasn't real. He couldn't stand another disappointment. 'You're a dream, aren't you?' he said warily.

She laughed softly, tucking her head under his chin. 'No, I'm real . . . Touch me . . . feel me . . . sniff me . . .' She pulled her head back to let him bury his nose in her throat. 'I smell nice, don't I? Even my sweat smells nice . . .' She giggled as he kissed her skin. 'Take me home . . .'

Belief began to seep through Alan. Belief and the first prickling of a wild, unquenchable joy. 'You little bugger,' he murmured, grinning, pulling her face down to his. 'You're not a dream . . .'

He was still grinning when he saw the line of light under the door, the box-like outline of the bunks opposite. It was a long time before he slept again.

4

Wednesday

Meet Mr McCool

A party was in progress.

It was a jolly affair where loud manly guffaws alternated with shrill feminine giggles. Music roared and glasses clinked. A voice, bright with enthusiasm, momentarily stilled the racket. 'Hi! Dicky Bird here. My parties are going with a zing this Christmas. Know why? It's new Party Mix, the drink mixer for every taste – in tangy, tropical four-fruits or smoothy tomato flavour. Yes! Gin, vodka and Bacardi taste new and exciting with Party Mix. Come in and join the crowd – with Party Mix –'

'Hey, Dicky, darling,' a girl's voice purred, low and breathy. 'Over here –'

'Excuse me, folks! See you later – help yourself to the Party Mix . . .'

As the sounds of jollity faded, Alan looked up for approval through the glass panel of the recording booth. Keith and a man from the commissioning ad agency were crammed into the tiny control room.

'Sorry, Alan,' said the engineer, glancing up from his console. 'We'd like to go again for the balance. We have to do a live mix.'

Alan swallowed his sigh. He didn't like performing in front of strangers – at least, strangers he could see. Normally he relied on Louis to keep his voice-over employers at a safe distance. They could be notoriously pernickety. But the ad man had been insistent. Alan pursed his lips as the man leaned over and murmured something in Keith's ear.

'... And Clive says could you make it a bit more suggestive at the end,' the engineer added, his zone muted with apology. 'Like you know you're going to have a good time ...'

Alan nodded glumly. The ad man resumed his steady gaze at the DJ. He was a dour, bespectacled individual with an accountant's eyes. The Superman insignia on the woolly pullover he wore didn't fool Alan in the least.

Keith faded up the party noises again.

'Hi!' Alan began. 'Dicky Bird here. My parties are going with a zing this Christmas. Know why? It's –'

'Hey, Dicky, darling –' the girl's voice broke in. Alan looked up in surprise as Keith killed the sound.

'Sorry, Alan. Wrong start mark on the tape ...'

This time Alan didn't disguise his sigh.

The wall clock in reception was nudging five-thirty

when Alan made a belated break for the outside world. He felt weary and jaded and still smarted from the ad man's blatantly insincere thanks for his patience as they finished on take twenty-two.

Nancy had to shout to attract his attention. 'A message for you, Alan!'

He back-pedalled to the reception desk. Nancy lifted up a scrap of paper.

'A Mr Bruno Culinari says he'll see you outside the car park at six o'clock.' Her tone hinted at intrigue.

'Mr who?' Alan frowned.

'Bruno Culinari.' Nancy handed over the note. 'He was dead weird.' Alan stared at the straggling signature. It meant nothing. 'Oh, and Alan. Bob Hope and Fred Astaire . . . The doubles competition,' Nancy prompted as he gave her a blank look. Two men rose from the seats facing the desk. They grinned expectantly at Alan, who smiled back thinly and then looked even blanker. Neither resembled anyone he had ever seen before.

'I'm Bob Hope,' the nearest helped him. He was a thick-set, pale-eyed man in a flat cap. There *was* a faint upward curve to his nose. 'I was actually more like him when I was younger – I've got a photograph. Do photographs count?' He reached into his jacket pocket.

'Well, I'm not sure. The rules are a bit vague on that score –' Alan flashed a swift call for help to Nancy who only smiled, quietly amused. A dog-eared snapshot was pushed under his nose.

'Look – that was taken in 1958. Everybody says that I was his double then. Surely that must go for something –?'

Alan glanced at it quickly. 'Ah, well, look – Bob – we'll let you know about that. Thanks.'

It was no good. He was in no mood for this. He turned for the lift.

'Oh, Mr Bird!' the second man called. 'Fred Astaire –'

Alan gazed, bemused, as the other executed a quick flurry of dance steps. He was tall and angular, owl-eyed behind heavy horn-rimmed spectacles.

'Smashing –' Alan breathed. The lift doors opened. He dived for them.

Disappointment flared in the two men's faces.

'I know Dicky'll consider it seriously,' Nancy covered for him. 'He'll certainly let you know.'

'Come *on!*' snapped Fred Astaire. 'It's only radio. Who's going to know the difference?'

'Yeah,' his companion nodded. 'Who's going to see Bob Hope on radio?'

'There should be a special category,' Fred added. 'For tap dancers –'

Nancy nodded sympathetically. 'Yes, I see your point.'

Bob Hope grunted and turned away. He had come up here for prize money, not sympathy. 'I feel like a wounded animal,' he told the rest of reception, which happened to be deserted.

Fred Astaire brightened. 'Will we get our expenses, anyway?' he asked. Nancy looked dubious.

'Bus fare?' said Bob Hope, turning back, hopefully.

*

Bruno Culinari.

Alan stared at the note as he joined the spiralling queue to the NCP exit. The name sounded suspiciously Sicilian. Could that be a link with the ice-cream war? The Mafia muscling in on Glasgow's ice-cream and raspberry essence trade? He grinned at the thought. Until the image of iron bars crashing through Mr Bunny's windows made him stop, suddenly uneasy.

His fears began to multiply as he paid at the kiosk and turned right out of the car park. To his left, parked at the end of the cul-de-sac which contained the stacker, was a van, whose headlamps flashed on and off as he appeared. It was an ice-cream van.

He slowed as the vehicle moved off and overhauled him. Its interior lights were on, but this time there were no fairy princesses on view inside. Three men sat in the back, gazing at him through the glass panel in the rear door, their faces unsmiling and pale in the artificial light. But, more disturbingly, all three were well groomed and smartly dressed, their ties neatly knotted, top coats well fitting. These were not the clothes of ice-cream vendors.

The largest, a broad, hulking fellow with deep-set eyes and a heavy black beard, gestured at Alan to follow. Alan poked his finger queryingly ahead. Blackbeard nodded sharply and gestured again.

Alan swallowed. He was not going to argue with this crowd. They didn't look the type to make do with iron bars or pick-axe handles. For all he knew there were sawn-off shotguns and automatic pistols tucked away among the wafers and cornets. As the van moved off Alan rolled obediently in its wake. It was a long journey.

Out from the city centre the odd convoy threaded its way roughly north-westerly. Office buildings and flyovers were left behind. Light industry loomed through the street lighting, then the marching columns of housing estates. Alan was back in ice-cream territory.

He tried to avoid the grim gaze of his guides, or guards, riding up ahead in their bouncing box of light. Instead his eyes picked out the lettering across the back of the van.

FOLLOW ME FOR
MR McCOOL'S FAMOUS ICES
The Number One Ice Cream

EXPERTS AGREE
Gold Medals Rome Turin Milan Naples Venice
Genoa Florence (1908) Taranto (1911)

Alan smiled mirthlessly at the friendly injunction.

Mr McCool. It wasn't any less bizarre than Mr Bunny. But the growing Italian connection worried him.

Only one of the trio in front appeared obviously Mediterranean: a lean, thin-faced man whose stare seemed more furtive than the others. He looked as if he would be good with a stiletto. Then, for some reason, Alan thought of the ice-cream princess. That rich black hair, the sloe-eyes, the fullness to her lips – he could imagine them curling in a look of scalding sensuality – could she be Italian too?

His memory of her occupied him to such an extent that the van's sudden leftward swing through a tall wooden factory gate caught him unawares. He wheeled quickly after it, and found himself in a shadowed yard, abruptly conscious of high brick walls pressing on either side. Ahead a large, elderly factory building reared into the dark sky. The only illumination dimly lit a canopied loading bay. The van drew to a halt against it. Alan slotted the Cabriolet in at its side. He had no idea where he was.

Apprehensively he waited in the driver's seat as his three guides piled out of the back door of the van and bustled over to him. To his surprise all three were grinning foolishly. Out of the harsh light inside the van they appeared absurdly young. As Alan rolled down his window Blackbeard bent down to him, nodding shyly.

'Thank you for coming, Mr Bird . . .' He tried to extend his hand through the window, but the angle was wrong and he made awkward, shrugging gestures of apology, his grin widening. Alan obliged him by opening the car door and stepping out. Immediately Blackbeard was pumping his hand. Alan smiled in return. The man was a kitten!

'It's a real treat to meet you, Mr Bird. This is my brother Paulo . . .'

A younger, chubbier version of himself stepped forward to grasp Alan's hand; without a beard his pink face appeared cherubic.

'. . . And that's Renato . . .'

The stiletto-wielder now looked simply thin and a little weedy. He was clearly the youngest.

He mimicked Dicky Bird's off-key whistle as he shook hands with Alan. The others giggled nervously.

'... And I'm Bruno,' Blackbeard finished. By now everyone was grinning. Alan felt he had stumbled on to an impromptu gathering of the Early Worm fan club. He didn't know whether to be flattered or make do with astonishment. Bruno resolved his dilemma. He gestured to a door at the back of the loading bay.

'Come inside, Mr Bird ... and meet Mr McCool.'

Inside Alan had the impression of space – the roof was high above their heads and their feet echoed ringingly against the solid floor. But the light was subdued, the view restricted by the proximity of huge, stainless steel vats. As they filed down a corridor between them, machinery hummed distantly. There was no other noise. The factory seemed merely to be ticking over for the night.

Alan saw only two workers – men in white coats and white caps who stepped back between the vats as the procession passed. Something in the way they moved struck a chord of recognition in him. But Bruno was forging ahead too briskly for Alan to have more than a glimpse.

At the end of the corridor they climbed a narrow steel staircase. Alan glimpsed the rounded tops of the vats receding into the distance, linked by high catwalks. Then he was through a door, moving across a broad, white-painted space where there were smaller, waist-high vats before a row of heavy steel doors. Bruno went directly to a further, normal-sized door at the far end.

They entered a large, gloomy office, its ceiling sloping to the longest wall where glass panes overlooked the factory floor. A desk stood against this wall. A tall, patrician-looking man rose quickly from behind it.

'Papa . . .' Bruno began, going over to him, and immediately launched into a flood of purely accented Italian. The seamless transition from broad Scots startled Alan.

He studied the new man as they talked. He was in early middle age, a handsome man with even, dark-jowled features, a face accustomed to responsibility, to taking decisions. His taut, slightly stoop-shouldered frame was attired in a blue-grey, superbly tailored business suit. A Godfather? Alan queried with a twinge of his old apprehension. But there was a quiet warmth in the man's eyes as Bruno turned suddenly, ushering Alan forward.

'Mr Bird, this is Mr McCool.'

'Mr Bird.'

Alan had half expected a dry, Brando-style husk of a voice. In fact it was rich and deep, though thickly accented; he chewed the Scottish vowels like sticky toffee.

They shook hands across the desk top – a firm, authoritative grip, not unfriendly. He was immediately business-like.

'I believe you know Mr Bunny –?'

The question caught Alan off balance. It had emerged as a statement, a presumption of a great mass of shared knowledge.

'Hardly at all . . . no,' said Alan, bridling. 'I bought a ninety-nine from him . . . we exchanged a few words . . .' He shrugged in the kind of exaggerated way that he thought might appeal to an Italian.

Mr McCool nodded briefly, as though digesting this. He indicated a chair at Alan's side. 'Sit down – please, Mr Bird.'

Alan sat. Behind him Bruno and his brothers gathered chairs and pulled them up close.

Mr McCool settled behind his desk. He put his hands together on the top. 'Mr Bird,' he began, 'ice-cream is an old-established business. Everybody knows where he stands – in the city. We all work together. It's a kind of family –'

Alan nodded. 'That sounds nice –' The comment sounded lame to him but he was anxious to appear co-operative. He had no idea where any of this was leading.

'Of course,' Mr McCool went on, 'everything depends on trust – kind of unwritten rules. A certain amount of honour is involved – But Mr Bunny doesn't play by the rules!'

There was a flash of concealed anger there which drew a nervous cough from Alan. He covered himself quickly.

'The unwritten ones . . .?'

'Yes,' Mr McCool nodded. 'It's a territorial thing, really. Other people work in the east, in the south, but we do business here, in the north, where we belong. But Mr Bunny –!' He snorted. 'He's all over the place, Mr Bird. He is an interloper – he's like a rogue elephant – wild – no rules –'

Alan thought it time to disassociate himself.

'As I say, we only exchanged a few words. In fact I'm not even sure if it was Mr Bunny himself –'

'No, no, no –' Mr McCool interrupted him with a brisk shake of the head. 'There *is* no Mr Bunny, Mr Bird. I told you – he's wild – he's a rogue – no family – no heart – just a bunch of desperadoes –'

Passions were rising a little too swiftly for Alan. He turned to appeal to the younger men, who listened in rapt silence. 'What's it got to do with me?' he asked.

Mr McCool answered. There was clearly only one man in charge here. 'You must talk to him. Get him to see reason – before things get bad.'

Alan stared at him, his interest fully engaged for the first time. 'But they're bad already,' he snapped angrily. 'My car! The seats are ruined! Have you ever tried to get ice-cream off velour upholstery?'

With a smack that made him jump, Mr McCool thumped the desk top. An impassioned burst of Italian followed, directed half at Bruno, half at Alan, who slumped back in his seat, his anger rapidly deflating. It was very difficult to argue in a language you didn't understand.

Mr McCool's outburst continued for a full minute, punctuated by more thumps, loud snorts and gestures of unmistakable derision. The only word Alan could recognize was 'Dicky'.

Eventually he ran out of steam. Alan looked lost, then Bruno leaned over his shoulder.

'My father says that things can only get worse if *you* don't help us. People do desperate things when their livelihood is threatened. For reasons of honour and for other reasons we can't talk directly to Mr Bunny. He will listen to you because you are a man of position. Everyone puts their faith in you. My father says he speaks for the whole of the ice-cream community . . . And my father asks if he can call you "Dicky" . . .'

Mr McCool had clearly only taken a breather. There was a fresh gabble of Italian, though quieter and briefer than before.

'My father says that ice-cream is his life,' Bruno translated. 'And he called you "Dicky" again.'

Alan was aware of Bruno's eyes lingering on him warily, as if anticipating a complimentary outburst. Then Alan understood. 'Oh – call me Alan. My friends call me Alan.' He paused. Nothing of this had turned out the way he had expected. But he had to admit that he was flattered. They clearly meant it all quite seriously. They were treating him – seriously. 'Well –' He couldn't help a faint smile of pleasure. 'I'll do what I can . . .'

The atmosphere changed abruptly. There were beams all round. Paulo and Renato appeared to be punching each other. Mr McCool rattled something off to Renato who dropped his guard and scuttled out of the room.

'Thank you for helping us,' Mr McCool told Alan. 'I knew you would. You came along just when we needed you.'

Alan's smile widened; it became bashful.

All four accompanied him on his return through

the white-painted area. The two workers Alan had noticed below were now standing at one of the small vats, pouring a red liquid into it. There was a dull thump from beyond a heavy steel door.

Paulo went to open it. Renato emerged in a sudden draught of frosted air. He was shivering violently, a tub of ice-cream in his hands. He gave it to Mr McCool who presented it to Alan. 'A small early token of our appreciation, Alan. Gold medal deluxe. Vanilla. But of course you can have any flavour you like.'

'No, that's fine,' Alan smiled. 'Vanilla's fine.'

'This is what Mr Bunny and people like him want to deprive the people of,' Mr McCool continued. 'First-class ice-cream.'

His sons nodded their agreement.

'Thank you,' said Alan. But the sight of the giant refrigerator had jogged his memory. 'I wonder . . .'

'Yes?' said Mr McCool.

'Could you help me out with a pint of milk? I think I've missed the shops.'

'Of course. Of course.' He spoke again to Renato who was blowing into his hands. With a worried look, the youngest McCool disappeared once more through the steel door.

The others moved on. As they passed the two workers Mr McCool waved at them with a paternal smile.

'That's Archie, and Amos. Two of my best men.' He pointed a finger at Alan. 'Dicky Bird from the radio!'

Alan nodded at the smiling faces. He was less certain now that he knew either of them.

'Actually, *I'm* Amos,' the nearer man corrected. 'He's Archie.' But the party had already walked on, hearing only belatedly repeated thumps from the steel door. Paulo hurried back. Renato caught up as they reached the loading-bay door. His fingers were blue as he pushed the milk bottle into Alan's hands.

'Here, let me pay for this,' said Alan, reaching for his pocket and fully expecting a polite rebuff.

To his surprise Mr McCool said quickly: 'Well, if you insist. It's twenty pence – just exactly what we paid.'

Alan had to juggle the bottle and ice-cream to search out the coins. He handed them to Mr McCool who thanked him and spoke in Italian to Bruno.

'My father apologizes for speaking in Italian,' said Bruno, 'but he says it is the language of his heart.'

Alan shrugged. 'Oh, sure –' All this flowery chat and talk of honour was beginning to make him feel awkward, especially when he had to pay full price for his milk.

It became clear that Mr McCool was going no further. 'Well, cheerio,' said Alan. 'And – thanks for the bottle . . . and the ice-cream.'

Mr McCool's hand shot out and Alan had to juggle milk bottle and ice-cream again.

'Goodnight, Mr Bird. Thank you very much.' With a curt nod he stepped back. One by one, with self-conscious smiles, the others shook hands too.

Bruno held the outside door open. 'Goodnight.

We'll keep in touch,' he told Alan as he passed.

Faces crowded the doorway as the DJ descended to the Cabriolet. With a final flurry of nods and waves they disappeared.

Alan opened the car door and put his milk and ice-cream in the back. It had been one of the oddest evenings of his life. He still felt a little bemused by it – but good. He really felt quite good.

He was just about to climb into the driver's seat when the loading-bay door opened again and a podgy figure hurried down the steps, waving a notepad. It was Paulo.

'Dicky! Dicky!' he called. He slid to a halt at Alan's side, his round face glowing pinkly. 'Can I have your autograph?'

Alan grinned. 'Yes, sure – have you got a pen?'

The young man fumbled in his overcoat pocket and produced a biro. 'Could you make it: "To my dear friend Paulo"?'

Alan mouthed the words as he scribbled them on the pad. 'That's a good Scots name there,' he added. Paulo giggled. 'Dicky Bird,' Alan finished. 'Tweet-twiddly-tweet.'

'Great,' Paulo breathed, retrieving pad and biro. 'Thanks a lot.'

Alan climbed behind the wheel. Paulo patted a wing. 'Lovely car,' he said admiringly.

'Thanks very much,' said Alan. In his newfound euphoria he had momentarily forgotten the outrage to his pride and joy. But if Paulo's remark contained irony, Paulo was quite unaware of it. As Alan drove out of the yard he glimpsed the young man's face in the rear mirror; it shone with undiluted pleasure.

An emissary. That was the word he was searching for. He rather liked the sound of it.

Alan spooned two measures of gold medal deluxe into one of his new bowls and put the tub away in the freezer. Then he poured himself a glass of whisky. He nudged the kitchen light switch off with his elbow and carried his supper through to the bedroom.

Emissary to the ice-cream trade. Well, why not? At least it was something useful, something *serious.*

What had Bruno said? People's livelihoods were involved. You could hardly say that about the Early Worm Show. And they had come to *him. Everyone puts their faith in you.* Alan had liked that. You couldn't shrug off that kind of responsibility, even if it dropped on your shoulders for the most capricious of reasons. Because of it he could almost forgive the damage to his car. Almost.

He sat on the bed, bending to deposit his bowl and tumbler on the carpet. As usual, most of his pullovers had dropped on to the floor during the night.

Perhaps this really was the new life he had been looking for. For the first time since Maddy's departure he was being given the chance to control his own destiny, to mould a viable future –

Then he picked up a faded burgundy sweater which had been kicked half under the bed and all thought of new lives vanished from his head.

The end stitching of a crocodile-skin handbag was just visible. With a quickening heart, Alan pulled the bag from the shadow of the mattress. He had been with Maddy when she had lifted this from a shop in Queen Street.

Inspiration struck him suddenly. Leaping to his feet, he heaved the bed sideways. A hand clutched at his chest.

The space beneath the bed was a treasure trove of Maddy's possessions, a forgotten repository for her magpie nature. Discarded head scarves and blouses jostled snapshots and tattered paperbacks; lipstick and eyeliner were entangled in a ball of tights; odd earrings cluttered a lone shoe.

It was as if she had been conjured up, voodoo-style; so much of her physical presence was here, exhilarating him and leaving him stricken at the same moment. Almost deferentially, as if examining the precious relics of a shrine, he picked through the pieces. Every object roused a different, heart-piercing memory.

It was a good two minutes before his masochism was glutted. He sucked in breath, lifting a silk slip to his nose. Maddy's perfume was thick in his nostrils.

He sighed abruptly, pushing back the bed and kicking the handbag out of sight with the rest. Only the slip remained. He draped it over the mattress next to him and gazed at it for long long moments. Then he pushed it under the pillow and reached for his whisky.

5

Thursday

In the hall of the ice-cream queen

'. . . So that's a definite decision, folks, reached by myself and the entire panel of judges, assembled here at enormous expense last night. The rule is: you've got to look like whoever you look like *now* . . . Not in 1910 or next year, but now – and only current photographs will qualify . . .'

With a flourish Alan faded up Gladys Knight and the Pips and reached for a cup of coffee with his free hand. He sipped quickly. This morning he was in a rare good mood, fully recovered from the hiccup of the night before. Purpose, he had decided, made a remarkable difference to a man's mental equilibrium. He felt closer to the silent hordes beyond his studio window than he had in a long time.

'I think our judges have reached the only fair decision,' he went on, easing back the music, 'and I know this will be very bad news for Bob Hope of Anniesland, but come on, Bob – keep trying –

maybe you can practise looking like somebody else! Which leads me on very neatly to something that's going to happen to me this afternoon. I've got to go and visit my dentist – ouch! – and he happens to be the absolute spitting image of a well-known Hollywood actor. No names yet, but I've got very big plans for my dentist in the Dicky Bird doubles match. So watch out Mr Dentist!'

Back came Gladys Knight. The studio clock read three minutes to nine. In the control room Keith was counting down the last thirty seconds before the commercials when the music suddenly faded again. As he looked up Alan leaned into the mike, his face oddly humourless. 'Before I go today I would like to steal the airwaves just for a moment and get a wee bit serious. I've got a message for someone who may be listening . . . Mr Bunny – or Miss Bunny – I do want to talk to you again, so how about the same time, same place tonight? End of message.' Instantly Alan's tone resumed its normal levity. 'And listen everybody: one day soon I'm going to tell you all about this, maybe even in a special programme. But until then, I'm a man of mystery . . . So that's all from your old Early Worm until tomorrow morning. Bye bye for now!'

He finished with his off-key whistle, beaming broadly. In the control room Keith had been joined by two of the production staff. 'Mr Bunny?' mouthed one. The engineer raised his eyebrows and shrugged.

Mr Roderick C. Nesbit, MA, LDS, RCS (Edin.)

did not look like the kind of man Alan would regard as a typical Metrosound listener. He did, however, closely resemble George C. Scott – a George C. Scott whose ultra-masculine energies seemed to have been diverted almost entirely into the mixing of dental amalgam.

Alan tried vainly to focus on the man's glistening forehead as he probed painfully at a suspect molar. Alan had been about to broach the subject of Dicky Bird's look-alikes when a routine scaling and polishing had grown unexpectedly complicated.

Roderick C. Nesbit clicked his teeth. He stood up. 'I'm afraid that tooth's very bad,' he announced in a soft Edinburgh accent. 'So what we'll do, seeing it's you, is pop a dressing into it and if there's no pain we'll probably be able to save it on your next visit. Now, when I've done, I don't want you to eat on that for at least an hour to give it a chance to harden. Okay?'

Alan grunted his agreement. With what felt like several pounds of cotton wool in his mouth it was difficult to respond in any other way. He decided to postpone the mention of look-alikes to a more suitable occasion.

It had been dark for almost an hour before Alan finally retraced his path to the scene of the assault on Mr Bunny. Rush-hour traffic and his own poor memory had delayed him – he had intended to be here in daylight and reconnoitre the area thoroughly in advance. But in the event he realized he might never have recognized the spot again without the cover of night. The housing scheme sprawled anonymously between two hills; one end looked much like the other.

He parked and waited, checking and re-checking the portable recorder at his side. As before, nothing moved under the amber glow of the street lamps. But for the odd lighted window, the low, wedge-roofed apartment blocks might have been abandoned years ago.

He felt pleasantly taut, ready for whatever action the evening might bring.

Half an hour later he was still ready, and a little peeved. The dashboard chronometer showed 6.21. He had assumed that Monday's encounter had taken place at around six. An assumption he had no way of checking. If, that is, Mr Bunny had decided to turn up anyway.

The faintest of chimes, trickling through the car's open window, convinced him otherwise. He cracked open the door. A distant 'Hello, folks . . .!' echoed out of the darkness.

Galvanized, Alan flicked the ignition and roared off in hot pursuit. The sound had appeared to come from directly ahead. But to his annoyance the road immediately began to twist and turn and finally climbed away steeply to the left. Alan was about to stop and turn back when he realized that the houses were thinning; he was reaching the top of a hill. It would be a good vantage point.

Pleased, he glimpsed the lamplit pattern of streets spreading in his rear mirror as he pulled off the road on to a grass verge. He turned off the engine and got out.

The estate filled the shallow valley below him,

a patchy grid of black and amber, speckled with house lights. Something moved towards the middle. But it was only a saloon car. Then a van nosed into view almostly directly beneath him. It was awash with light, chimes tinkling up the hillside. Turning at the end of a cul-de-sac. He had it!

His blood up, Alan flung himself back into the driver's seat, gouging lumps of turf as he swung the Cabriolet in a tight circle. He went back down the hill at sixty, swerving off at the first left turn. He turned left again at the first junction, then braked heavily as the road suddenly narrowed to a walkway, guarded by bollards. A further road was visible beyond it, running at right angles. As Alan watched, Mr Bunny's van trundled into and out of view, a truncated 'Hello, folks . . .!' chirruping in its wake.

Alan swore under his breath, snapped into reverse and shot backwards into the junction. The swine was trying to run for it. Well, let him try. He was dealing with an investigative journalist now, not a mob of impassioned ice-cream vendors. He righted himself in the middle of the junction, then shot straight ahead. Almost immediately there was another crossroads. As he braked he glimpsed the rear of the ice-cream van disappearing round a curve in the right-hand branch. Missed again!

But the road up ahead curved in the same direction. Could the two branches form a crescent? The thought of snaring the man from an unexpected direction, skidding across his bows, appealed to him. Grinning, he gunned the engine and sped onward.

Houses peeled back on either side. The road continued to curve. It was bending back on itself. He had been right. But where was Mr Bunny?

He saw the side turning at the same moment the ice-cream van pulled out of it into his path. He stamped on the brakes. Parked cars lined the road; there was no room to swerve; he knew he was going too fast. He glimpsed a look of horror on the van driver's face. Then there was a bang. Not a satisfying crunch of rendering bodywork, not even a squeal of tortured metal, simply a tinny thump like two buckets knocking together.

Suddenly Alan was staring at the mangled wreckage of his right wing.

Stunned, he disentangled himself from his seat belt and got out. There was no doubt of it. The whole wing was buckled like crumpled silver paper; the edge of the bonnet was bent inward; a headlamp had gone; the front bumper was almost in two. He couldn't believe how he had allowed this to happen. The magnitude of irresponsibility, of blind, reckless stupidity overwhelmed him.

Something dropped out of the air, brushed his shoulder and hit the bonnet with a bump. It was a large rubber rabbit, modelled in a legs-crossed position, with long, pointed ears, two monstrous buck teeth and an absurd grin. Vaguely he remembered it decorating the roof of Mr Bunny's van. Its sudden appearance seemed entirely appropriate.

Mr Bunny was studying the buckled radiator and bumper of his van. He was wearing the same bomber jacket as on Monday, but his tam-o'-shanter sat at an odd angle, his square face was pale and blank-eyed. He looked as overwhelmed and incredulous as Alan. 'This is the reserve vehicle,' he murmured. 'All the rest are in the bodyshop. This is me completely out of action. No more front-line units . . .'

'I just wanted to have a word with you,' Alan offered.

'I know that!' the other snapped. 'I was coming to you – where did you think I was going?'

'I thought you were trying to get away –'

'Oh God almighty!' Mr Bunny raised his eyes skyward, making Alan feel even sillier than he did already. 'This was my best night on the Loganville estate. I was clearing up here –' He grunted and ran a hand over the Cabriolet's broken wing. 'At least your radiator's okay. I'll get the lads at the bodyshop to beat this out for you.'

'No!' The thought horrified Alan. 'No, I'll get it fixed.'

Mr Bunny reached over the BMW's bonnet and picked up his rubber namesake. 'Well, no point in hanging around here, is there? Come on – follow me back to HQ.'

Glumly the two antagonists retreated to their wounded vehicles. Warning lights winked on the dashboard display when Alan switched on the ignition. They hinted that all was not well with the headlamps. But the engine fired easily enough. He heard nothing drop on to the road as he went into reverse. It was small enough consolation.

Steam curled from Mr Bunny's radiator as he backed into the side turning, then turned. With a visible judder, the van led Alan into the night.

*

The Bunny HQ was surprisingly close. A row of elderly tenements fanned into a broad industrial avenue. A huge yard piled with car and lorry tyres, warehouses to let, a single-storey factory building, silent behind grubby railings. The ice-cream van swung through an ornate iron gateway and halted before a wide, roll-up door. Mr Bunny hooted. A covering moved away from a window to the left and a face peered out. The door rolled up.

Alan followed the van into a huge, brightly-lit area of furious activity. It was like stepping suddenly into the hold of an aircraft carrier during a pitched battle, except in place of damaged fighter-bombers were more than a dozen battered ice-cream vans. Acetylene torches flared everywhere, hammers crashed, drills whined. An army of boiler-suited repairmen were hard at work.

A couple came over to Mr Bunny's van as Alan climbed out of his car. Behind them the roll-up door rattled down again, hiding the scene from prying eyes.

'You've seen some action tonight, Trevor,' one commented. 'Was it a ramming job?'

Mr Bunny – Alan decided that Trevor suited him better – jerked his head in the DJ's direction. 'No, it was Robin Hood here – coming to rescue me!'

The repairman nodded. He was a short youth with tousled hair and a foxy look. His eyes fastened on the Cabriolet. Then he noticed Alan.

'Oh, you're . . .' The young man mimicked Dicky Bird's whistle. Alan nodded. The other grunted and aimed a Dr Marten's at the BMW's wing. Alan was still registering shock when he did it again. 'Just superficial damage,' the repairman remarked casually. 'I'll get Roddy to bash it out and slap some paint on it . . .'

'No!' Alan cried. 'Please – I'll fix it tomorrow.'

The young man shrugged. 'Suit yourself. But it'll cost you a fortune to get it repaired anywhere else.' He turned to Mr Bunny. 'We can field two units tomorrow night, Trevor. I've patched up the freezer on the Merc.'

'Good! Well done,' said Trevor. 'Listen, is Charlotte . . .?'

'In the office,' the young man finished. Trevor moved off.

The repairman joined Alan again in silent contemplation of the Cabriolet's desecration. 'So,' he said at last, 'is this the ultimate driving machine, then?'

Alan could think of nothing to say. A shout from across the bodyshop distracted him. Trevor was beckoning. He waited until Alan reached him and they started walking towards a small, glass-sided office at the back.

An unusually crisp 'Hello, folks!' made Alan turn his head. In a corner two men stood at a xylophone. One, tall and bearded with hair like a toothbrush, was playing the Mr Bunny tone. His stocky companion was mouthing the Mr Bunny phrase into a small cassette recorder. If Alan hadn't witnessed it he would not have believed it. Then he remembered his own recorder, lying unused in the car. He was debating whether to go back for it when a slight, dark-haired, smiling figure appeared in the office doorway in front of him. Instantly he forgot all about tape recorders.

It was the ice-cream princess.

Alan's heart was doing racing turns. He tried not to stare as he followed the girl inside. She was perched on high heels, her slim legs swathed in dark cord; a man's grey pullover hung from her shoulders; heart-shaped earrings dangled from a high-piled froth of hair. She looked – *edible*.

'Take a seat,' Trevor invited. There was only one. Alan sat, crossing his knees. Something odd snagged the corner of his eye. He turned. He was sitting in front of a shelf packed with rubber bunnies, each mirroring his stance. He uncrossed his knees.

'Mr Bird here wants to talk to us,' said Trevor. 'He's seen McCool.'

'Oh yeah?'

The girl spoke with such calculated insouciance that Alan was quite shocked. His mental picture of her had been one of sweetness and light, tinged with the teeniest hint of corruptibility. Suddenly this young woman didn't seem like that at all.

'McCool wants to get together – reach an agreement,' he said uncertainly. 'He's very upset –'

Trevor and the girl exploded into brittle laughter. The girl began a flowery and disturbingly accurate imitation of Mr McCool delivering his 'ice-cream is my life' speech, complete with gestures. At least Alan thought that was what it was; her Italian accent sounded native. After a moment he started to feel annoyed; he seemed as much the butt of the joke as McCool.

'I think it's a serious offer –'

'Oh McCool's serious all right,' said Trevor, snapping off the humour. 'He's deadly serious.'

The girl spoke again rapidly in Italian, her eyes hard. Trevor listened intently, nodding quickly, while Alan performed some more mental readjustment. Could she *really* be the ice-cream queen? The brain behind Mr Bunny? The prospect intrigued him. Trevor turned back to him suddenly.

'Do you have any idea of what you're getting involved in? Do you work for McCool?'

'Certainly not,' said Alan, annoyed at the suggestion. 'I'm a journalist. I'm trying to stop senseless violence.'

Trevor and the girl exchanged looks. It seemed to dawn on them that Alan was not quite what he had appeared either. Some of the brashness went out of Trevor's manner.

'McCool runs a big outfit –' he started to explain.

'And he wants to talk,' Alan broke in.

'He wants to *annihilate* us, is what he wants!' The vehemence of the outburst made Alan flinch. 'McCool's got a stranglehold on every independent operator in the north of this city. He controls every franchise – wafer supply – ice-cream – soft drinks – he's even got a ten per cent mark-up on every gallon of raspberry essence. And if you do your shopping elsewhere then you get the demolition treatment –'

The girl interrupted with a flood of Italian that sounded no less vehement. Alan blinked at her uncomprehendingly.

'How long have you been locked up in that radio station?' Trevor asked when the flow paused.

'Do you have any idea what's going on around here?'

Before Alan could reply the girl resumed her flow. Most of it seemed to be directed exclusively at Trevor. Alan didn't know whether to be grateful or irritated.

'You see,' Trevor continued at last, 'your Mr McCool is the unacceptable face of big business around here. You look at what big business has done to this town – it's screwed it, it's left it lying in the shit with its bum in the air! Well, those days are gone, because now it's every man for himself.'

All these bilingual onslaughts were beginning to wear on Alan. 'I got the impression,' he tried, 'that he just wants to find a working relationship . . .'

'Yes! Exactly!' Trevor laughed mirthlessly. '*Us* working for *him*!' He stabbed a finger in the direction of the bodyshop. 'Do you want me to go out there and tell those people that *you* want them to go and work for McCool? After the threats, the violence, the day and night work here? *You* go and tell them!'

It was Alan's turn to laugh. 'Well, something's got to be done,' he cried. 'It seems so – stupid – it's almost like a joke. People getting so angry about ice-cream! It's a joke . . .'

'Oh yes?' Trevor snapped. 'And what deadly serious occupation are you engaged in, Mr Dicky Bird? What exactly is your contribution to humanity?'

That stung. Alan's mirth subsided. He paused. 'I want to help – but what can I do? I want to help all of you find a solution . . .'

Trevor snorted. 'Well, that's very noble of you, Mr Bird.'

The girl began to talk again, in a quieter, more business-like way than before. Trevor listened in silence. Eventually he nodded and waved a hand at Alan.

'You tell McCool this: we'll take his ice-cream, but under *our* conditions. Every Mr Bunny is his own boss, and that's the way it stays. We're talking equal prices with no mark-ups – and an open market in wafers – we buy where we want. If he prices fairly then he gets the business. Now on territories we are willing to negotiate openly around the table. We talk under those conditions.'

Alan had nodded throughout this, conscious that he was being led into commercial realms that meant nothing to him. He disguised his ignorance by asking what seemed to him a harmlessly technical question.

'Where do you get your supplies from at the moment?'

Dark looks passed between Trevor and the girl.

'So that's what McCool's after!' Triumph flashed in Trevor's eyes. 'Is *that* why he sent you?' He nodded at the girl. 'He must be worried, Charlotte –'

'Nobody sent me,' Alan cut in.

'Okay,' said Trevor. 'Well, go back to where nobody sent you from and you tell him what we've said. We talk in an open market!'

Alan sucked in breath. He was beginning to see why Common Market negotiators were paid so much. He shrugged. 'Okay.'

Trevor accepted his resigned tone with

equanimity. Some of the tension drained from the atmosphere. 'Right, you better go now,' he said, 'before the boys get to work on your car – you'll end up with a fridge in the back and a set of chimes!'

The thought did not strike Alan as entirely fantastic. He got to his feet.

'Charlotte, see Mr Bird off the premises,' said Trevor.

He was alone with her. Alone with his fairy princess. The ice-cream queen. Assuming, of course, he forgot the dozen or so bustling acolytes who hammered and banged on every side. But they were too busy to notice him.

She walked slightly ahead of him. Slinked rather, with a natural swaying motion that was as sexy as it was unforced. Alan was grateful for the view, but at the same time piqued by the galling, tantalizing phenomenon of an utterly desirable young woman who showed not the slightest interest in speaking to him.

'Er, *parliamo non*, er, *italiano*,' he fumbled.

'I speak English,' she said easily, but without slowing down.

'Ah – well –' he grunted, catching up with her with a swift, skipping step. 'I'm on your side, Charlotte,' he declared, 'you know that.'

Why did he always seem to be rushing after women?

But she did pause then, glancing at him with an amused, mischievous look. 'Oh,' she said.

Alan shrugged, smiling – he was sure – rather

more inanely than he had intended. 'Well, I'm on both your sides, really . . . because I think you should all be on the same side . . .'

She nodded, offering him no help at all. He couldn't tell if she was giving him his chance or simply enough rope to hang himself. It was the hardware department all over again. He could feel the prickle of sweat.

'I'd really like to see you again – I'd like to get to know you better.' He could hear ancient gears grinding in the remark. Could it really have been as bad as it sounded to him? Evidently it had been. The girl's face seemed to be having trouble containing a snigger; her eyes sparkled with a savage delight.

'What's the matter?' said Alan defensively. 'Don't people date each other any more?'

The snigger changed magically into a broad and brilliant smile. But its brilliance was a barrier excluding him. 'Well, gee! I don't know – shucks,' she breathed with a kind of withering mock coyness. It totally flummoxed Alan. Before he could even begin to react she had added a crisp, 'Bye bye,' and waltzed off.

Alan was suddenly aware that the xylophone in the corner was playing his jingle. He looked up. Trevor was at the keyboard.

'. . . always-gets-the-bird,' Trevor finished with a flourish and tight grin. 'Oh Mr Bird,' he called, tossing down the beaters and coming over. 'When you see McCool be sure to remind him –' He moved to a nearby van and thumped the wording on its side. '*Formerly* Mr Softy. No more!'

Alan watched carefully as he resumed his

approach. It had only just dawned on him that the relationship between Mr and Miss Bunny might be more than purely business. Which, now he came to consider it, was an oversight on his part of staggering proportions. At least it helped to explain her icy cold-shoulder, and the grim look currently hardening Trevor's features, which were sharp enough already.

He was doubly surprised, then, when Trevor suddenly produced a small white plastic tub from behind his back and shoved it into Alan's hand.

'Here – some ice-cream for you,' he said gruffly.

Alan broke into a hesitant and grateful smile. 'Thanks very much.' It was about time something nice happened this evening.

Trevor responded with a curt nod. There were clearly limits to his largesse. At the moment Alan was not inclined to try stretching them.

Cradling the ice-cream, he turned toward the Cabriolet. And instantly his face fell. 'Oh in the name of –!'

The foxy-faced repairman and a companion were eating fish and chips off the crumpled metal of the bonnet.

'We'll be finished in a minute, Dicky,' the young man reassured him through a mouthful of haddock. He smiled genially and continued chomping.

There was no problem about contacting Mr McCool. He was in the phone book under McCool & Co, Qulty Ice Cr Mfrs. Alan dialled and was put through to Bruno. A rendezvous was arranged for half an hour's time.

Alan stepped out of the telephone box, even further fazed by the night's events. If communication with the McCools was that easy, why was he involved?

Nothing of this made any sense. The closer he looked the more complicated it grew. No one was telling him the whole truth. He felt used and emotionally bruised. And the ice-cream queen was only the most tender part of it.

But he *was* involved. Whatever he felt, the two sides of this insane dispute still regarded him as important. That was an obligation, and in a perverse way he was grateful for it. He just wished someone would tell him what was really going on.

Mr McCool's café straddled a busy junction in Kelvingrove, an island of bright light opposite the darkness of Kelvingrove Park and the Gothic shadow of the museum and art gallery. In mid-evening it looked empty, the broad pavement outside deserted by pedestrians. Alan went in under a giant, neon-lit ice-cream cone. A small counter just inside was unattended. Then he saw the McCools squeezed round a table behind a formica-clad pillar.

Mr McCool saw him at the same time. He half rose and waved. 'Oh, hello, Mr Bird! Please come in – sit down.'

He ushered Renato out of the seat opposite and, nodding, Alan took it. He found himself facing Mr McCool and Bruno with Paulo to his right; Renato hovered at the table behind him.

The seats were cramped and hard, covered in patched plastic.

'Have a cup of coffee,' Mr McCool invited. He beckoned in the direction of the counter. A matronly woman in an apron materialized.

'Have you cake or some chocolate biscuit? Alan?'

'Yes, please,' said Alan, who had forgotten about food this evening.

'Maria,' asked McCool, 'what have you got left? Any Kunzle cake?'

'Yes, I have two Kunzle cakes, and some apple pie,' the woman replied.

'Oh good, good, good.' Mr McCool was either nervous or suffered from a passion for sweetmeats; his fractured accent made it difficult to tell. 'Mr Bird and I – we have the Kunzle cakes. Some biscuit for the boys. Five cappuccinos. Oh, and a wee slice of apple pie too – that's a good girl.'

The woman nodded and went. Bruno looked peeved. 'I wanted some Kunzle cake too,' he said.

'Well, that's a pity, Bruno,' said Mr McCool sharply, 'because you'll just have to have some apple pie or a Yo-yo, won't you?'

Bruno looked suitably abashed, but Alan could see resentment simmering below the surface. All of them seemed oddly subdued, tense. Were they afraid he had found out something he shouldn't?

'So, Alan,' Mr McCool went on, 'what did Mr Bunny have to say for himself?'

'A lot,' said Alan. 'He wants to talk. I think it could work out good.'

McCool nodded non-committally. 'Where did you meet? His place?'

'We went there, yes.'

'Where? Where is it?'

Alan felt all four strain for his answer; this was privileged information.

'Now, listen,' he said tartly. 'I'm not taking any sides. You asked me to help you *talk* to Mr Bunny. That's all.'

McCool's face darkened, but at that moment the coffee and cakes arrived. The tension slackened as plates and steaming cups were distributed. The boys took their chocolate biscuits; Alan had to lean to one side as Renato reached forward for two. Then he saw Bruno eyeing his Kunzle cake covetously.

'Hey, Bruno, please,' he said, offering it. 'Have this.'

Gratefully Bruno accepted it.

'Bruno.' Mr McCool spoke quietly without turning his head. 'Give Alan his Kunzle cake.'

Bruno's face fell. Without a word he handed the cake back.

Alan accepted it without demur. If Bruno and his father were playing silly games, that was their business. He stirred his coffee while the others sipped in silence. 'They have simple demands,' he continued. 'They want to do business with you – that's obvious.'

'They?' Mr McCool interrupted. 'Who's they?'

'I spoke with Trevor. That's no secret, is it?'

'Trevor?' McCool's eyes widened. 'Trevor! Trevor! Trevor!' His palm slapped on the table, releasing a sudden flood of native invective, his face reddening in anger. Prudently Alan leaned back to sip his coffee. He was beginning to get used to these Mediterranean explosions.

There was a hiatus when the outburst finally ended. Bruno looked up calmly.

'My father says of all the most loathed names you have to mention that one – the most abhorred name of all. The name of a two-timing interloping fish and chip seller – a name without honour – the name of a son whose father turns in his grave to see the disgrace that he brings to his family . . .'

Alan frowned. 'I don't understand.'

'Trevor is a Marinetti,' Bruno explained. 'They have fish and chip shops all over. We were close to them at one time. Then Trevor started to drift into ice-cream. He shouldn't have, because there was a kind of –'

'Unwritten law?' Alan finished with a trace of irony. The more he heard about honour in this context the more suspect it sounded.

Bruno nodded.

Alan picked up his Kunzle cake and took a bite. Instantly he squealed in pain. 'Forgot . . .!' he mumbled through a mouthful of crumbs. 'I was at the dentist today.' He swallowed and put down the cake, wincing and massaging his molar through his cheek. Bruno's eyes fastened on the abandoned Kunzle.

'What else happened at Mr Bunny's, Alan?' Mr McCool asked, composed once more and plainly unmoved by the spectacle of human suffering.

'Nothing much.' Alan wiped moisture from his eye. 'He wants to talk, that's for sure. And he gave me some ice-cream. Just like you did.'

'Ah. That's nice.' McCool's eyebrows lifted. He turned to Bruno. There was a brief exchange in Italian, rapid but apparently without rancour. '*Si, papa, si,*' Bruno finished.

Alan looked at him for a translation. Bruno simply drank his coffee. As the silence lengthened into embarrassment, Paulo's eyes began to flicker between Alan and his brother so rapidly in the end that Alan glanced at him questioningly. It was a rare opportunity for a younger son to show his mettle.

'My father says that one taste of that ice-cream could answer very many questions. My father has the taste buds of a master. He knows every ice-cream in the country. He –'

'Paulo!' Bruno snapped suddenly. '*Silenzio! Imbecille! Stazitto! Idiota!*'

Paulo blushed and looked aghast.

Alan nodded. He had heard enough to realize what was going on. He stood up. 'You're not having my ice-cream, Mr McCool. If you want one there's a Mr Bunny van every night up in Possilpark –'

'Alan – please sit down – have another coffee,' said Mr McCool quickly. But Alan was already moving toward the door.

'Just let me know when you really want to talk,' he called back. 'I'll be happy to fix it up for you. *Ciao*!' And he had gone.

Mr McCool breathed out with a soft, hissing sound that made Paulo sink even deeper into his seat. Bruno gave him a withering look, then transferred his attention to Alan's Kunzle cake. As he reached out his hand for it his father snapped loudly, 'Bruno! No!'

Alan set his Mr Bunny tub next to Mr McCool's gold medal deluxe in the back of his freezer compartment. There was plenty of room. He kept nothing else in there.

The tubs looked identical; only the labels on the lids differed. If he had any sense, he told himself, he would throw them both away and forget he had ever had anything to do with two gangs of ice-cream-crazed Italians. He could settle straight back into a comfortable, well paid, untroubled existence, carefree, sharing his life with whomever he pleased. Like Charlotte . . .

He shut the freezer door with a thump. *That* was too sore a point for the moment.

But it underlined his true situation. He wasn't carefree. Maddy had made him carefree – for most of the time – and he didn't have Maddy any more. All he had now was a dented BMW, two tubs of ice-cream and a fast multiplying set of problems that showed no sign of going away.

He sighed and reached for the whisky; there were only a couple of inches left in the bottle. They would have to do.

The crash was so sudden and so close that Alan shot up in bed, blinking and confused in the darkness. If it was another Maddy dream it was the most convincing yet.

He had just begun to persuade himself that he *had* been dreaming when it came again. Softer, but unmistakably inside the flat. A second later a light showed beneath the door.

Alan swallowed, feeling the hairs rise on the back of his neck, his heart start a slow, reverberant thunder.

Outside, a faint shuffling sound continued; a gentle rustling that could have been a human whisper; a sharp click. Alan was rigid, torn between a desperate desire to burrow under his makeshift bedclothes and an even more terrifying urge to throw open the door. Instead he prayed that his eyes and ears were somehow mistaken, that his terror would miraculously purge the flat of intruders.

Then the shuffling ceased. There was an endless silence. Abruptly the light under the door went out. A heavier click than before, that could have been the latch on the front door, cut through the blackness.

More silence.

Alan was still straining his ears for sounds, too frightened to get up or lie down, when he fell asleep.

6

Friday

'You're a dead man, Dicky Bird!'

The alarm woke Alan at the usual time. The severe crick in his neck reminded him of the night's excitement. His upper body was lying parallel to the headboard, where he had slumped, his legs twisted below him.

Wincing, he got up, massaging the back of his neck. When he felt moderately human again, he cracked open the bedroom door, listened, then padded quietly through to the living room.

He had a shock when he saw the light in the kitchen. Then he realized that any ambusher would be visible through the frosted-glass screen.

He went in. The striplight over the main work-top had been left on. Alan distinctly remembered turning it off the night before. Just as he had shut the door to the freezer. That was open too, and Mr Bunny's ice-cream offering had gone.

*

'... And I'm saying this for any Mr Bunny who may be listening. The message is urgent. Mr McCool is on the trail. Be prepared! Mr McCool is on to you. So, please, same time, same place, Mr Bunny and I'll give you all the details. But in the meantime – double the guards, send the women and children to the hills!'

Keith exchanged worried glances with the three members of the production staff who had joined him in the control room this morning. The Early Worm's increasingly eccentric messages were beginning to create interest. Keith had been overseeing Alan's show for nearly two years now and he had never heard this note of over-excitement, of genuine agitation in the DJ's voice before.

Neither had Hilary Sandeman.

The MD rose, frowning, from his desk and moved closer to his office's monitor speaker as Alan drew the show to a close.

'So till tomorrow, this is Dicky Worm your Early Bird saying cheerio ... And don't forget prize day tomorrow on the Dicky Bird Doubles Match. I can tell you that the big prize this week is a wee bitty special. It's one whole day's use of station boss Hilary Sandeman's American Express card. Knowing our Hilary, he'll make it Boxing Day when all the shops are shut, but never mind, you'll just have to make the most of it, big winner, whoever you are ... And finally, once again I have to get a bit serious. Mr Bunny, if any Bunny is listening out there then please get the word back to big Mr Bunny – the McCools are on the warpath. Bye!'

Hilary reached for his internal telephone.

'Gloria,' he said quickly, 'I want to see Alan Bird.' He slammed down the receiver.

Alan was pleased with his broadcast. Of course it wouldn't solve all his problems. But it was a start. He was taking an active part at last, instead of simply being vandalized, burglarized, traumatized . . .

He was fed up with being everybody's else's pawn. Well, that was going to change. *He* would make the moves now – bang some heads together if necessary.

He felt good about his new mood. His new life was shaping up at last. He was beginning to see things as they really were. He breezed into reception, nodding to Nancy and Murdo, the station's tame minister who was dropping in his taped Christmas Eve meditation.

'Ask Keith to stick fifteen seconds of *Silent Night* by Elvis on the front,' Alan heard, and paused in mid-stride. A small, dark-haired man in an expensive windcheater was sitting opposite the reception desk.

Alan blinked at him, a smile forming. The day was really looking up. The man's resemblance to Dustin Hoffman was extraordinary.

'Oh, Nancy,' said Alan, turning. 'Sorry, Murdo.' He nodded over his shoulder. 'Is this one of mine?'

'Oh, yes, Alan –' Nancy began. But Alan was already turning back, moving across reception with a broad smile of encouragement. 'It's good! It's very, very good!' he told the seated man. 'I think I can safely say a weekly winner – maybe even a monthly topper! Congratulations – it's really very, very good.'

The man gazed at him blankly.

Alan was interrupted by a concerned-looking Nancy calling, 'Alan, can I talk to you a minute?'

'Really spot on,' Alan finished, bunching his fist. He went back to the desk.

'Hilary wants to see you,' Nancy told him.

'Right.' Alan shook his head delightedly. 'They're getting better, eh? Just one or two like that and it makes the whole thing worthwhile. It'll really encourage the others, too. Great . . .'

'Yes, well, Hilary did say straightaway,' Nancy said.

Alan grunted and headed off toward the administration corridor. As soon as he was out of sight, Nancy turned toward the seated man and treated him to her most deprecating smile.

'The features editor will be just one more minute, Mr Hoffman,' she said.

Gloria showed Alan straight through to Hilary. The station's MD was pacing up and down in front of his window.

'Morning, captain,' Alan greeted him brightly.

Hilary halted with a disturbed look. 'Alan, I heard the show – what was all that about?'

'The charge card?' Alan shrugged dismissively. 'Oh, that was just a gag.'

'No, no, not that.' Hilary indicated a chair; Alan sank into it. 'I mean the other thing – about Mr Bunny. Now what's going on?'

'I told you – I'm on to something.' What had

prompted this odd mood in his lord and master? Alan thought they had settled all this on Tuesday. 'It'll break soon. I'll make a programme.' He smiled reassuringly.

Hilary seemed far from reassured. He settled on the edge of the desk, peering with furrowed brow at his employee.

'Alan, you have not been yourself lately –'

'No, that's just the point!' Alan agreed at once. 'I *wasn't* myself before – when you *thought* I was myself. But now I *am* myself – or very nearly.'

Hilary's furrows deepened. 'I don't follow you.'

'Look, I told you – I'm changing. I had to. My life was the wrong – flavour – like my whole life was the wrong ice-cream. It needed a new flavour!'

Alan was grinning at the obviousness of it. He was glad he had popped in. Hilary plainly had a knack for helping him clear his thoughts. It was a rare gift.

'Ice-cream?' the MD enquired warily.

Alan nodded excitedly. 'You see, I was raspberry when I should have been – vanilla. Do you get it?'

'Oh –' Hilary tried to chuckle, thought better of it and coughed. 'Alan,' he asked, 'does this Mr Bunny talk to you a lot?'

'Oh I talk to them all – I see them all,' Alan said easily. 'I'm helping them – they need me.'

'Them all?'

'Yes!' Alan leaned forward to emphasize his point. 'I needed to care for something – to get involved. You can ask my friend Colin. He's a surgeon.'

Hilary pursed his lips. It was worse than he had feared. He had clearly caught Alan just in time.

'I've got a friend, too, Alan, who's a kind of a doctor. Would you like to have a talk with him?'

'What about?'

'I think you should see someone soon, Alan, someone who can help you find yourself . . .'

Alan frowned. 'You mean a psychiatrist, don't you? You think I'm nuts. I'm not nuts!'

But Hilary was adamant. 'Before you go on the air again, Alan,' he said with the kind of solemnity he normally reserved for the discussion of salaries, 'I'm going to have to insist . . .'

The psychiatrist's address was in Broomhill, one of a gentle crescent of ornate, four-storey Victorian terraces, so imposing yet so indistinguishable that Alan had to run up and down several steep stone entrance steps before he found the discreet brass plate he was looking for.

A scratchy-voiced entryphone admitted him to a cool, tiled hallway. The psychiatrist's office was at the end.

Alan still wasn't entirely sure why he was here – beyond the pistol Hilary had applied to his head. He was going through a crisis, certainly; he was far from happy and he could do with a lot more sleep and a lot less whisky and ice-cream. But frankly he had seen Hilary acting more bizarrely than he was on numerous occasions.

As he knocked on the office door, however, he found himself too curious to be annoyed. He had often wondered how a genuine trick-cyclist operated.

A brisk 'Come in' ushered him into a cramped, well-ordered room full of dark wood and worn leather. Important-looking tomes mingled on the copious shelving with intricate models of ships, rolled charts, a sextant. Paintings and photographs of vessels of all kinds crowded what little space remained on the walls. A ship's bell hung over the fireplace.

The man who turned and smiled a reply to Alan's cheery 'Afternoon' was wearing a heavy polo-necked fisherman's pullover. He was kneeling beside a small side-table adjusting the rigging on a large model of a four-masted schooner.

'Mr Swan?' he said, without getting up.

'Bird,' Alan corrected.

'Make yourself at home. I'll be with you in a jiffy.'

Alan took a longer glance round the room. Most of the heavy tomes, now he looked closer, appcarcd to havc nautical titlcs. At least there was a proper leather couch against one wall. He sat down on it and stretched out; it was very comfortable.

'I wouldn't lie there,' the psychiatrist said mildly. 'That's another twenty pounds an hour.'

Alan grunted and got up again; he could imagine Hilary's reaction to that.

'It's mostly used for group therapy nowadays, anyway,' the psychiatrist went on, rising to his feet.

Alan chuckled out loud. The psychiatrist smiled amiably; he was a small, thin man with wiry, grey-streaked hair that looked wind-ruffled, and a fleshy, curiously precise mouth. He showed Alan to a chair beside a roll-top desk. They both sat.

Alan's gaze wandered to a book at the corner of the desk top. He read the title upside down: *Cruising in Strange Waters.* He looked up to find the psychiatrist gazing at him speculatively.

'So, I hear you have a friend called Mr Bunny?' he asked.

'Yes – not a friend – somebody I'm helping,' said Alan. 'I'm helping all of them, all the Mr Bunnys.'

The psychiatrist nodded and smiled. 'How long have you been associating with these Mr Bunnys?'

'All week. Since Maddy left.'

'Maddy?'

The psychiatrist's smile seemed somehow to have stuck, become some kind of odd facial manifestation that bore only the most tenuous relationship to the needs of the conversation. Alan decided to ignore it.

'My girl,' he explained. 'She left me. We'd been together for four years. It was – a bit of a shock.'

The psychiatrist scribbled something on a pad; he was still smiling. 'How did that happen?'

'A removal truck came one night – she left. It was very sudden.' Alan drew in breath. 'Quite a shock.'

The psychiatrist was scribbling again.

'How was your relationship with Maddy?'

'It was fine,' said Alan, rallying. 'Well, *I* thought it was fine.' He smiled. 'I thought we were a very good team.'

'Did you have a healthy sexual relationship?'

Alan nodded. 'Very healthy – I thought.'

'Any abnormal sexual practices?'

Alan hesitated. What was abnormal these days? He'd once been out with a girl from Cambuslang who thought that sticking his tongue in her ear was the height of carnal indulgence. But that was years ago . . . He and Maddy had just enjoyed themselves; in fact she'd usually been the one who thought of anything new. Memories were prompting a smile when he became aware that the psychiatrist was staring at him fixedly.

'No,' he said.

'Nothing at all?'

Alan shook his head. 'No.'

'Any sexual violence?'

'Certainly not!'

'Very well. We'll take your word for it.' The psychiatrist's smile nearly vanished. He was clearly disappointed. 'So, tell me,' he went on, 'how do you feel about losing Maddy?'

'Heartbroken.' Alan grunted. 'It was – terrible. It was a big shock. And I've had these dreams, these awful, depressing dreams . . .'

'Dreams?' The other brightened visibly.

'But now I see it's all for the best,' Alan continued. 'I've already explained this to Hilary – I think that we've all got to change at certain times. If your life is like a – an apple cake, when, for instance, it should be like a Kunzle cake, then you're in trouble! You've got to find the right flavour. Maddy and I – we were like a chocolate mousse . . . we were a really terrific chocolate mousse! But you can't live on chocolate mousse.

No, you need other things –'

Alan grinned, pleased with this supreme effort of explication. Perhaps a pyschiatrist really had been a good idea, after all. But then he remembered the reason for it all. 'I do miss Maddy, though. She was wonderful.' He sighed. 'We were *some* chocolate mousse . . .'

He lapsed into silent reverie. The psychiatrist put down his pencil and pushed aside his pad. There were no rich pickings here.

'I wonder if you've ever done any sailing, Mr Bird?' he asked after a pause.

Alan shook his head.

'I have a little illustration that might be of some comfort. It goes back to my days in the Navy. They used to move us medicos around a great deal – ship-to-ship – and they had this contraption called a breeches-buoy. Sometimes you could find yourself out there on the ocean –'

'Between the two ships,' Alan broke in enthusiastically. 'Just hanging on a piece of rope – there's nothing else around you but the angry waters – you're stuck between here and there – oh, yes, I know, I know. You're right!'

The psychiatrist gaped at him, smile wiped clean. 'How did *you* know that?' he snapped. 'That's *my* story.'

'Oh,' said Alan, 'I'm sorry.'

'It's *my* story,' the other repeated. 'It really happened to me! Where did you hear it?'

Alan shrugged. 'I don't remember. Maybe I read it in a book.'

'No you didn't.' The psychiatrist was growing petulant. 'I haven't written it in a book yet.'

Alan shrugged again; he couldn't think of anything else to say. 'I'm sorry.'

'This is very upsetting.' The other man was fumbling nervously with his pencil. 'It really happened to me, you know,' he said, looking up suddenly, his eyes bobbing like corks in a high swell. 'It really happened. I didn't make it up –'

Alan nodded encouragingly. 'I believe you,' he said. 'I really do –' He felt awful.

It was a good ten minutes before Alan was able to leave the man. Finally he had become disgruntled and subdued, mumbling something inaudible about his bill and retreating to his model schooner. As Alan eased the door shut he heard the parting twang of catgut rigging and a soft curse.

Tinged with guilt as the visit had been – he really should have come clean about Hilary's piece of plagiarism – Alan was not unhappy about having made the effort. Confession *was* good for mental equilibrium. He'd had no idea how much progress he'd made on the Maddy situation before he had begun talking; he was even quite annoyed the psychiatrist hadn't let him go on. But, of course, he didn't need to – not here, at any rate. He already had a perfectly good doctor. One who would be as pleased with his progress as himself.

He jumped into the Cabriolet and went in search of Colin.

'. . . But McCool himself – what a rogue! He takes

the biscuit. Imagine – he can taste any ice-cream and he'll tell you precisely who made it and where. What a palate!' Alan shook his head, his eyes bright with wonderment.

Rather less enthusiastic, Colin grunted, half his attention on the clipboard of patient data sheets in his right hand.

'I'd be more worried about his arteries than his palate if he's been living on ice-cream all his life,' he commented drily.

They were walking down an apparently endless, sloping corridor at the rear of Colin's general hospital. Colin was grateful for its length. Alan had caught up with him just before he had turned into it, on the last stretch of his afternoon rounds. But for that the surgeon might have been less inclined to slip into his father-confessor mode. He had been up since six and it had been a wearing day. On the other hand, Alan was a friend – and an increasingly agitated one to judge by his current behaviour.

'I've got to warn the Bunnys tonight.' Alan's expression was suddenly grim. 'I think the McCools could be on to them . . .'

The abrupt change of mood finally persuaded Colin to abandon his clipboard. He halted and faced Alan. 'Listen,' he said, 'what about Maddy? It's only been four days now. I think you should take a little bit longer than that to get over her – after all she meant to you. I don't think you're being very fair.'

Alan snorted. 'Oh, don't worry! I'm still miserable – I'll be miserable for ages, I know. But I can see the way forward now.' His eyes glittered.

'The ship on the horizon . . .'

'The ship . . .?' Colin echoed.

'Oh yes.' Alan nodded, and moved on.

At the end of the corridor a sign reading 'Female Surgical' headed a pair of swing doors. Colin led the way into a bright, busy ward. He went straight to the bed of an elderly, elfin-faced woman who sat up against her pillow sipping tea.

'Hello, Miss Wilson. How are you today?'

'Oh fine, doctor.' The woman lowered her cup and smiled brilliantly. 'Just a bit stiff.'

'I'll tell Sister you can have a real bath today, then.'

The woman almost cooed with visible delight. Alan watched the brief exchange, struck by his friend's bedside manner – a subtle mix of briskness and benevolence, leavened with a careful irony that prevented either from becoming too serious. It was a neat trick. He could do with it on the air. Then he realized that Colin was smiling at him.

'I've brought someone to meet you. Dicky Bird from the radio. He's a friend of mine.'

As Alan moved closer, the woman leaned forward, her eyes shining. 'Very pleased to meet you, Dicky! This is a real treat! I listen to you every morning here. I'm always awake first, and they don't bring breakfast until half-past seven.'

Alan grinned, embarrassed and touched by such unabashed enthusiasm. 'Well, thank you very much. It's nice to know you're here – or you're there – out there listening, I mean –' He chuckled to cover his verbal clumsiness and the woman joined in the joke.

'I wish you did Saturday and Sunday, too. They've got that other noisy clown on then.'

'Ah, yes, Rufus.'

Miss Wilson shook her head. 'I don't like him.'

'I don't like him much either,' Alan agreed. They chuckled again, wrapped in an instant conspiracy which Colin was obliged to dissolve.

'We have to go now,' he reminded Alan. They said their goodbyes.

'Cheerio, Dicky!' the woman called after them. 'You make an old lady smile. Every morning!'

With a final wave Alan followed Colin through a door at the further end of the ward. They found themselves in a broad service corridor, lino-floored and echoing, against the outside wall. Alan was still folded in the warmth of his reception. Miss Wilson was the first fan he'd met in days who hadn't threatened him with an iron bar or vandalized his property.

'Is she a kidney lady?' he asked at last.

'No, she's a plastic hip lady,' Colin told him. They began walking.

'How long has she been in for?'

'A couple of months.'

'Jesus –' Alan grimaced.

'Oh, she's okay,' Colin reassured him. He grinned. 'She's got you.'

Something made Alan glance at his friend; the surgeon wore that wry look which invariably hinted at deeper meaning, or perhaps simply commented ironically on the lack of it. Alan didn't have time to make up his mind. They had reached the door to the car park.

'Well, anyway,' Colin went on smoothly, 'you've

obviously got a great deal to do and you shouldn't really be here unless you're sick.' He cocked an eyebrow. 'You're not sick, are you?'

'No, not really.' Alan shook himself and laughed. He was surprised at how nervous it sounded to him, but he was already opening the door. He turned back. 'Thanks, Colin. I'll be seeing you.'

'Keep on taking the alcohol,' the surgeon advised. Alan grinned. He went out into the gathering dusk.

He was early for his evening rendezvous and he took a round-about route, tempted to open up the Cabriolet and see if the damage was still restricted to the bodywork alone. But he rejected the plan as reckless. An expert should look under the bonnet first and he hadn't even had time to arrange a garage appointment. The thought of how many Thrifty Pops and Party Mix ads would have to pay for the repairs was soul-destroying.

Instead he tuned into Metrosound – loyalty forbade anything else – and found himself listening to the Friday arts review. Carol MacNeice, 261's cinema correspondent, was interviewing Dustin Hoffman about a new film. Alan's pulse quickened as he realized the star was actually in the city. The coincidence struck him as heaven-sent. If he could get the actor on to the Early Worm Show with his prize-winning look-alike – perhaps even making the award himself . . . What a coup!

He was making a mental note to grab the features editor as soon as possible when he spotted the entrance to the ice-cream estate. As he turned under the familiar amber street lamps all sense of elation flew out the window. He was immediately tense, watchful, sucked back into a crazier, harsher world whose denizens brandished iron bars as freely as ice-cream cones, whose war chariots could leap out of the gloom and commit casual mayhem on thirteen thousand pounds of engineering excellence without a glimmer of conscience. Old outrage stirred within Alan – as much against himself as the ice-cream warlords. The sound of crumpling Cabriolet would be carried to his grave. Making deep personal commitments to a cause was all very satisfying emotionally but he hadn't quite counted on this kind of expense. It was hardly unreasonable to look for some kind of tangible return. Like Charlotte . . .?

Potentially intriguing as this speculation was, he put it aside, aware that his attention was straying from the way ahead. It wasn't only Mr Bunnys he had to look out for, he reminded himself. The McCools could just as easily have responded to his all-points bulletin. But as he inched from junction to junction, driving rather more carefully than he had in earlier days, he saw no sign of ice-cream activity, heard no echoing chimes through his half-lowered window.

Twenty minutes' patrolling brought him to the hill-top vantage point he had discovered the previous evening. He turned on the grass verge and parked, killing the engine and winding the window fully down.

Oddly, for the first time since he had visited the estate, he noticed hints of occupation: two or three cars whining along roadways, odd figures dotting the pavements, a horde of BMX bikers congregating at a junction. He thought of dazed populations emerging from the bunkers after bombers had moved on. And a suspicion popped into his mind. Did this really indicate something? Had the ice-cream war shifted ground yet again – naturally with no one bothering to tell him of the changed situation?

Irritation sharpened his suspicion. He had dropped at least half a dozen record requests to make his Early Worm appeals this morning. It was nearly seven by the dashboard clock. By rights the place should have been swarming with flop-eared Mr Bunny trucks a good thirty minutes ago.

Scowling, he twisted the ignition, stamped the accelerator and swerved away in the direction of the Bunny HQ.

He rolled through the iron gateway and halted just outside the roll-up door. As before, the building looked empty, until he rapped smartly on the slatted metal. A face appeared in the window to the left. Alan recognized the foxy-faced repairman. Then the door rattled upwards and he ducked inside.

There seemed slightly fewer vans than the night before, but, if anything, the frenzied activity had increased. The young repairman heaved the door down again, tossing his head in the direction of the nearest van. Through a white mist of acetylene smoke, Alan glimpsed Trevor on the rear step.

'Trev!' he called, hurrying over. 'I've been

waiting hours. Didn't you get my message?'

Trevor frowned. 'What was that?'

Alan sucked in breath. 'McCool got hold of your ice-cream. He reckons he can track you down.'

To Alan's astonishment the other man burst out laughing. 'Oh I don't think he'll get too far,' he said.

Alan looked at him blankly.

'It's his own recipe,' Trevor cried.

At the same instant Charlotte appeared from inside the van, popping her head over Trevor's shoulder and grinning slyly. 'McCool's my father,' she announced with a kind of vicious glee.

Alan blinked. The war hadn't shifted ground; the combatants had. Or rather, it now turned out, they'd been entrenched in positions he hadn't even realized were there. 'I don't get it,' he murmured, confused. Then he began to. McCool's enraged outbursts, Charlotte's, the weird obsession with honour . . . This wasn't about ice-cream or livelihoods – it was a sordid, stupid little family quarrel. And it had already cost him his car, his peace of mind, perhaps even his job – 'What are you *playing* at?' he demanded, the anger surging within him, until at the sight of their broadening, heedless grins it burst out in a rush: '*You're all crackers!*'

Trevor and the girl cackled wildly, as if they truly were demented. 'Nothing like a family feud, Dicky, is there?' Trevor roared.

'Crazy people!' Alan said, red-faced with frustration and humiliation. 'You're all crazy people!' Both sides had duped him in almost every possible way; his sense of justice, of fair play, his egotism, his sexual interest, all had been ruthlessly guyed. No wonder Charlotte treated him like a clown. Ice-cream wasn't the joke. *He* was.

Just as the cackling threatened to become unendurable a heavy thump echoed through the building. Abruptly the laughter cut off. Taut glances flashed between Trevor and Charlotte. Heads turned across the bodyshop.

The thump came again, its origin and its effect suddenly clear. The roll-up door had buckled under a massive impact. As drills whined to silence, torches sputtered out, the lowest door slat bent inward. The tip of a crowbar appeared, dug into the concrete floor and jerked violently, snapping the lock. With a rending crash the door peeled upwards, ripping from its guide chains and swinging free. An abrupt silence followed, punctuated only by the soft creaking of the shattered door.

For a frozen moment Alan thought he was dreaming. The dozen or so crouching men who now filled the gaping doorway looked like figures from a nightmare, acolytes of some demon king. Their clenched fists bristled with a ferocious and unlikely armoury: bicycle chains and pick-axe handles, hammers and crowbars, a wooden mallet of Thor-like proportions, a modern hunting crossbow. But their faces registered as much astonishment as those inside, as though the sudden violence had startled them all equally – until a burly man at the front let his pick-axe handle sink through his fingers and clink against the concrete, once, and then again. Then a second man struck the floor with the tip of an iron bar. The mallet-wielder joined him. A clamorous din spread, ragged at first but growing swiftly more rhythmic, until the building rang with it, a crude, clattering, bellicose racket of defiance. Over it Alan suddenly heard Trevor shrieking at him. 'You brought them here, you bastard! You're a dead man, Dicky Bird! You're a dead man!'

Then, with a shout, the intruders charged. Instantly the scene dissolved into chaos. Fist fights and wrestling matches developed across the floor; windscreens and headlamps shattered under hammer blows; metal rang against metal.

Terrified, Alan stepped back behind the van. Something whistled over his head and landed with a soft thud. A rubber bunny bounced at his feet with a crossbow bolt through its neck. One look was enough. Discretion was the better part of self-preservation. For all he cared the McCools and the Bunnys could happily massacre each other.

He rounded the van and aimed for the door by a circuitous route. On either side McCools worked hard to destroy ice-cream vans and the Bunnys worked harder to stop them. He side-stepped two white-spattered antagonists duelling with paint sprays. A noise as of a collapsing xylophone was followed by discordant chimes, hiccuping 'Hello, folks!', then a confused medley of assorted melodies from *Jingle Bells* to *Lili Marlene*. In Trevor's van he glimpsed Bruno and Charlotte screaming at each other, gesticulating wildly in a bizarre Italianate semaphore of abuse. Outside lurked Paulo, glancing round with a look of cherubic malevolence before seizing the van's headlamp and vainly trying to tear it loose.

Madness. They were all certifiable. Every last one of them . . .

An unguarded gap appeared at the door. Alan seized his chance and ran.

The Cabriolet's door cut off the noise of battle. Hurriedly Alan switched on the engine and reversed to turn. He was not fully straightened when a sudden roar from behind drew his eyes to the rearview mirror. A mob of enraged Bunnys, led by Trevor, were pouring through the body-shop doorway. Suddenly they were all around him, kicking at the BMW's tyres, hammering its bonnet and wings with spanners and mallets, stabbing and ripping its canopy with screwdrivers and knives.

Cold horror seized Alan, and even colder outrage. He squeezed the throttle, inching forward through the torrent of blows and abuse, gazing fixedly ahead as Trevor pressed his face to the driver's window, spittle flying from his lips in an extremity of rage.

'You're a dead bird, Dicky! You're a dead bird! *Bastard!* I'll roast you! I'll eat you! Nobody bucks a Bunny! Nobody . . .'

With a final crash against the boot, Alan was free. As he accelerated into the street he caught sight of the Bunnys turning and charging back inside, weapons raised. A cry of *'Andiamo!'* faded on the night air.

He bumped to a halt outside his apartment block, only realizing as he took his hands off the wheel that they were shaking. His whole body was shaking.

Too many emotions were jostling inside him. Hopes, dreams, expectations, illusions, all were blasted – the derision in Charlotte's face, the *hate* in Trevor's. That was all he had achieved, that and an explosion of Tom and Jerry violence.

The insanity of it, the galloping ice-cream lunacy of it all . . .

And his car . . .!

He lifted his head and saw street lights through the canopy. Scratchmarks sparkled in the rear windows. White grooves marked the bonnet as if it had been savaged by some monstrous tom.

The liquid trickling down his nose was a surprise. Then, as he tasted the saltiness on his lips, the logic of tears was suddenly perfect, and inescapable. He lowered his head on to the wheel, pressing his forehead hard into the leather padding. He hadn't cried for years. He hadn't even been able to cry for Maddy. But now he could.

The front door was unlocked. As Alan tried to use the key, it opened in front of him. Inside, the hall light was on. Feeling a knot of sick fear twist in his stomach, he moved his head round the door jamb. If the Bunnys had somehow got here before him, or the McCools had left a reception party . . .

The whole flat was ablaze with light. Then he heard dishes clatter from the kitchen, a drawer rattling shut – cooking sounds . . . No, it was too much to hope for. Not after all this time, after a night when the whole world had gone bad –

Squashing fear, he moved quickly through the hall, across the living room, into the kitchen doorway. The sigh started from the pit of his stomach, from the depth of his depression, rising, blossoming into a smile that glowed.

'Oh Maddy . . .' he breathed.

She glanced up from a cooker of steaming saucepans, smiling briefly. She was wearing a loose, dark red, kimono-style dress, one of his favourites. Her hair was bunched up high, leaving wispy, red-gold curls on the back of her neck. She looked – beautiful.

'I telephoned Colin,' she said. 'He said you were in trouble.'

Alan sighed again and slumped against the door frame. 'They attacked the car. A whole mob of them. It's wrecked!'

'Oh Alan –' Her lips tightened sympathetically; then she brightened. 'Are you hungry? Shall I fix you some eggs?'

'Oh yes –' Alan gasped. 'Yes, please – I'd love an omelette. I've been living on ice-cream all week.'

Maddy turned back to the cooker. 'Why didn't you get all the pots the same colour?'

Alan shook his head. 'I just wasn't thinking straight –'

'We'll go back tomorrow and change them. Okay?'

She smiled at him quickly. He smiled back. He went on smiling. Even though he knew she had to be a dream he couldn't tear his eyes away from her.

'Okay –' he whispered. 'Okay, Maddy, okay –'

The pain began as a crick in the neck, on the opposite side to the crick which had greeted him this morning. Then he felt a band of pressure across his forehead.

Grunting, he lifted his head from the Cabriolet's driving wheel, hearing the rumble of tired blood as it sluiced past his eyeballs. His gaze focussed on the dark windows of the apartment block. He was too weary, too overwrought to let disappointment touch him deeply any more; from now on he would let it wash over him, run its course until it no longer had any effect. But that was no reason to give it encouragement. He couldn't face the flat tonight – whatever surprises it held.

Shuddering fully awake, he turned on the engine, swung the wheel and clattered off in search of a bolt hole.

7

Saturday

Six hundred million Chinese can't be wrong

Sleepily Alan unglued an eyelid. A cat-sized Tom, painted in lurid colours, loomed over him with an upraised hammer. He blinked rapidly.

Then he saw the mouse-size Jerry scurrying at the cartoon figure's feet. Alan closed his eyes again and groaned. He knew exactly how the mouse felt.

After a pause for cogitation he sniffed and raised his head from the pillow. Morning sunlight filled the bedroom of the Misses Semple. He had never seen it in the light before. A frieze of cartoon characters marched above his small bed: Snoopy and Woodstock, Snow White and the seven dwarves, Tom and Jerry, Goofy. It reminded him of the battle at the Bunny HQ.

Across the room there were snuffles and grunts from the girls' bunks. Quickly Alan reached for his trousers. He had no wish to share his toilet with an inquisitive six-year-old.

Pushing his feet into his shoes, he stood up, easing on his shirt and making for the door.

'Thanks for the bed, ladies,' he murmured, softly in case he woke them.

'That's okay, Dicky,' Lily replied sleepily.

'Okay, Dicky . . .' echoed Sarah from the lower bunk.

Smiling, Alan went out.

'They used me – they all *used* me!' Alan cried, thumping the polished pine of the kitchen table for emphasis. 'They could have picked up the telephone if they wanted to talk to each other . . . And the girl! All along it turns out she's McCool's daughter . . .!'

'Do you want two eggs, Alan?' Colin asked in a tone that counselled rather more calmness than his unexpected guest was currently demonstrating. He nudged a second boiled egg across the table towards the first which Fiona had placed in front of him a good five minutes ago.

'Oh, no. Thanks, Colin, no,' Alan muttered distractedly. Refreshed from his night's rest he was too busy rationalizing the events of the previous day. Unfortunately, it was a process that both Colin and Fiona found equally baffling, sinee in the course of his excited outpourings Alan had yet to include a coherent account of what had actually happened.

'All the best fights happen inside families,' Fiona offered from the Aga.

'Yeah.' Alan snorted. 'That's what Trevor said – shortly before he demolished my car . . .'

Sarah and Lily, scrubbed and fresh from the bathroom, sidled through the kitchen door. Lily slipped on to a chair opposite Alan; Sarah climbed laboriously into a high chair. Both regarded him quietly.

'I just don't see any hope for the world.' He shook his head frowning. 'If people want to damage each other over ice-cream – we're doomed . . .!'

'I don't know,' said Colin, lightly cudgelling the egg Alan had declined. 'I think ice-cream's quite important. Isn't it, girls?'

'Yes,' lisped Lily. Sarah simply nodded.

Colin glanced up at Fiona. 'Did you pay the milk bill this morning?'

'No. You paid him two weeks last week.' She placed porridge bowls in front of the two children.

'I wasn't here last week, love,' Colin pointed out.

'Oh Colin, you said you were going to!'

'I *told* you –'

An argument ensued. In a moment it was heated enough even for Alan to notice. As his eyes flickered warily towards the combatants a restorative silence was abruptly imposed. Fiona turned back to the Aga.

'She's got two brothers, this girl?' Fiona enquired after a suitable pause.

'Three,' Alan nodded.

Fiona smiled. 'Well, that explains her rebellion anyway.'

'That's what got McCool really angry,' Alan resumed, his eyes flashing. 'His daughter mixed up with a fish and chip family – he's mortified!'

'Ice-cream and chips!' Lily suddenly declared from her porridge.

Colin and Fiona laughed, grateful for the intrusion of childish sanity. Only Alan remained grave.

'No,' he decided, reluctantly. 'It couldn't work . . .'

Lily's face was bright from the reception her comment had had. It was time to press her advantage. 'You said you'd get me a request today, Dicky,' she reminded him.

Alan's face fell. 'God, so I did! I'm sorry, Lily. I'll fix it – don't worry. I'll go into the station straight after breakfast. Rufus'll let me on for a minute or two.'

Colin looked at him carefully. 'You watch out for the ice-cream men,' he warned. There was only the hint of an irony Alan was in no mood to catch.

'Mm,' Alan grunted, looking down at his undamaged egg and spotting it as if for the first time. 'But I've got to do something about them – they're all so *angry* they can't even think straight.'

To Colin's mind the anger seemed just as much Alan's – a diagnosis that was immediately reinforced by the decisive way in which the DJ finally seized his spoon, raised it above the helpless shell on his plate, paused as if to take aim, then brought the implement crashing down. It was just as well that Colin was not telepathic. The image that had flitted across Alan's mind at the moment of impact had been that of Trevor's snarling face.

It was Alan's first sensible conversation with Rufus Dann in three years and they were arguing. Somehow Alan had always suspected they would.

'Let me into the studio for just one minute, Rufus,' Alan pleaded, holding a finger up against the control-room glass. 'Just to say hello to a kiddie and an old lady in hospital. That's all –'

Perched in Alan's very own studio chair, the Saturday Show man was unmoved.

'Sorry, Alan. I'd have to clear it with Hilary first. I don't know what happened between you two yesterday. I'd have to clear it –'

'You're a shit, Rufus!' Alan cried. 'I let you on to my show on Mother's Day, remember? Just because you hadn't phoned her for three weeks –'

From the monitor speaker Metrosound's own keep-fit lady – the Tartan Goddess – made impossible demands over a disco background. Rufus's engineer, even younger than Keith, kept his head well down at Alan's side.

Rufus endured his colleague's glare for almost ten seconds. 'Just give me the names, Alan,' he sighed. 'I'll take care of it.'

'Okay. Okay'. Instantly Alan was scrabbling in his jacket pocket for the note he had made of Lily's request. He found it. 'I'd like one for Andrew from Lily, but don't mention her name. And for a Miss Wilson in the Western Infirmary – just lots of love from me. Okay?'

'Which ward?' Rufus asked.

Alan frowned. 'I don't know which ward.'

Rufus nodded. He scribbled down the names. 'I'll play them something nice, Alan. No sweat.'

'No heavy metal, please –'

Rufus nodded again and bent his head to the live microphone as the Tartan Goddess faded into exhausted silence.

'Well, after all that exercise let's all sit down and think about a nice fattening pudding. And here's Katie Pollock with today's recipe. It sounds delicious – banana fritters. Mm . . . I can't wait . . .'

Yes you could, thought Alan, glaring again. *A request only takes two minutes.*

A curiously youthful female voice chirped from the monitor. 'Hello, everyone! Banana fritters – that's something you've probably seen on menus in Chinese restaurants along with other exotic things like ice-cream fritters, but they are surprisingly easy to make and so very different they're worth the effort . . .'

Something altered in Alan's expression. Threads of thought connected. He turned to the engineer.

'She said ice-cream fritters.'

'Sorry, Alan?'

'Katie Pollock – she said ice-cream fritters.'

The young man glanced at him, slightly uneasy. He was a good friend of Keith's and had heard rumours of Alan's mental state.

'Yeah, that's right,' he said warily. 'Like baked Alaska.'

Something odd was happening behind Alan's eyes; they shone. 'How do you make them?'

The engineer shrugged. 'Ask Katie Pollock –'

'Well who is she? Where is she?' Alan was beginning to throw his hands about. 'Is she a real person?'

'I don't know if she's a real person but she's Hilary Sandeman's wife –'

Alan was running down the corridor, past the studios, past the DJ's office, into reception. He snatched up Nancy's phone, went to dial, paused and rifled the little book of phone numbers she kept under the reception desk. Finding what he wanted, he started to dial again. While the tone purred he drummed his fingers on the counter top. A distant receiver clicked.

'Hello, Hilary! Yes – Alan – yes, much better. I feel fine. I think everything's going to work out fine. Oh yes!' He gave a brittle laugh. 'The angry seas are subsiding . . . I really phoned about something else, Hilary. I wanted to speak to Heather – do you know, I never realized she was Katie Pollock –' He caught his breath, nodding the seconds away, while Hilary lavished praise on his wife's culinary expertise. 'Yes, I wanted to ask her for a recipe, Hilary,' Alan resumed at last. 'No – just a recipe . . . Pardon? No, I'm fine. Honestly. Everything's cool – I'm in good shape – but I *do* need a recipe from Katie – I mean, Heather. And it's quite urgent.' He transformed a sigh into a polite laugh. 'I swear to you I'm on top of the world, Hilary.' He nodded. 'Yes, it's a *specific* recipe . . .'

Ice-cream fritters. Ice-cream fritters! The words drummed through Alan's brain as he negotiated the Saturday shopping traffic along Byres Road. On the seat next to him lay Katie Pollock's recipe, scribbled on a sheet torn from Nancy's telephone book. Complete but for one essential ingredient. Alan's eyes raked the lines of shops.

Why on earth did he never keep notes from his shows? After all, the man he was looking for had been a three-times winner in his Early Worm ethnic jokes competition.

He smacked the steering wheel in frustration. For God's sake, how many Chinese supermarkets could there be in Hillhead?

Then he glimpsed the Chinese symbols on a sign up ahead on the left. Not a restaurant, not a take-away. This was it. Smiling, he drove past until he reached the first kerbside gap and slotted in between the parked cars.

Over half an hour had passed before Alan could decently make his exit, declining a second cup of herbal tea and a third pancake roll, waving good-bye to the round-faced proprietor, his diminutive wife, their two small children, her midget-sized mother. He walked briskly the fifty odd yards to the Cabriolet.

The three Bunnys were leaning casually against the bodywork, looking quite unconcerned but making it equally clear that no one would be leaping inside and driving off without their express permission. Alan recognized the xylophone duo; he didn't know the third man.

It would be most unfortunate if his sudden brainwave ended in a bloody-nosed street brawl. It would be almost as bad if his potential assailants had seen why he had chosen to park here. But as he studied them more closely, swerving under a confectioner's awning to do so, he realized that the nonchalantly watchful way they scanned the busy street was genuine rather than assumed. They hadn't the faintest idea from which direction he was likely to appear. It had clearly been the Cabriolet which had attracted their attention.

Alan frowned and filled his lungs. This was not the moment for his courage to evaporate. The waiting trio weren't carrying spanners or screwdrivers and their overalls didn't bulge suspiciously. If the worst came to the worst he could shriek as loudly as any mugging victim. But it wouldn't. Anger bolstered his wavering resolve – anger at last night's final depredation of his car, anger at a week of threats and lies and deceit, anger most of all at himself for still allowing himself to be intimidated by this motley band of ice-cream maniacs.

He was seething by the time he moved from the shadow of the confectioner's. Remembered scenes of humiliation and defeat sparked through his mind like sequences in a badly edited film. If by some feat of foresight and dexterity he had been carrying three large ice-cream cones he would have derived enormous pleasure from plunging them, one after the other, into the three unsuspecting faces. Instead he brushed straight past the tall, toothbrush-haired xylophone player before the other had a chance to realize who was jostling him.

'Hey!' the man began. 'Trevor wants to see you –'

'Oh, no, pal,' Alan cut in, wrenching his key in the door lock. He grinned at the three men mirthlessly. 'No, you've got it wrong. *I* want to see *Trevor.* Oh, and just one other thing –' A fierce gleam came to his eye. He moved back a step into the road, lifted his foot and kicked the front wing heavily enough to add another dent. 'From now on,' he snapped, a look of peculiar satisfaction on his face, 'if anybody hits this car it'll be me, and nobody else. Now get in!'

The Bunnys exchanged curious looks, but they did as they were told. Elbowed out of the way by Alan, toothbrush-hair was obliged to bend almost double as he squeezed into the rear seat. As the car drew away from the kerb, he straightened, his head popping through a massive rip in the canopy.

'Sorry about the draught,' Alan murmured over his shoulder.

There was no more need for concealment at the Bunny HQ. The windows were unshielded and the doorway gaped open. Alan drove straight through, bumping unheedingly over a scattering of metal slats and squeaked to a halt.

The interior looked like a scrapyard, an ice-cream vans' burial ground. Not a side panel was undented, not a windscreen unshattered; twisted metal, ripped tyres, broken glass littered the floor.

Trevor stood in the middle of it picking desultorily at a pile of debris. For the first time Alan saw him without his tam-o'-shanter. His hair was uncombed; there was a large tear in the sleeve of his bomber jacket. He appeared to be quite alone. There was no sign of Charlotte, Alan noted with interest. Trevor glanced up with red-rimmed eyes as Alan got out of the car and walked over. This was a far cry from the enraged Bunny who had promised to roast him the night before. He looked pale, subdued, shocked into an unnatural meekness.

Close up, the transformation shocked Alan almost as much, but he sat heavily on an involuntary twinge of compassion. All this proved was that natural justice did exist after a week's evidence to the contrary. It was about time Trevor realized that too.

'So,' Alan said, 'it's gone about as far as it can go, eh?'

'Yeah –' Trevor's voice was no more than a whisper.

'What does *honour* demand now?' Alan snapped, unable to resist the dig. '*Hara-kiri*?'

Trevor hunched his shoulders. 'I just wanted to tell you. I don't blame you for anything that's happened.'

Alan's laughter echoed across the building. 'Thank you!' he cried. A fat lot of good compassion would have done here: the man's arrogance was incredible.

Trevor gazed at the DJ uncomprehendingly, the irony quite lost on him.

Alan recovered himself and prodded Trevor's leather jacket with a sharp finger. 'You and I are going to see Mr McCool,' he said firmly. He was beginning to enjoy a sense of power that was as unfamiliar to him as submission was to Trevor. 'I've got something to say to both of you. Fix it.'

Trevor looked uncertain. 'How?'

'Phone the bastard! Or would you rather send a war party . . .?'

'What will I say?'

Alan sighed. After numerous displays of arrogance and Mediterranean fire, Trevor was beginning to reveal the mental agility of a *crème glâcée*. It was almost heartening. 'Just tell him that I want to talk to him, that's all. He'll turn up.'

With a look that suggested compliance only because its owner could think of nothing better to do, Trevor turned and shambled off toward the vandalized front of the office. Alan shook his head. He cast an eye round at the aftermath of battle. His Bunny escort had vanished, presumably to where Bunnys went in the daytime. The scale of destruction that met his gaze made even the Cabriolet's desecration look reasonable. But that was an unworthy thought. To make amends he aimed a kick at the pile of debris Trevor had been examining. To his surprise something hidden clicked into motion. Then, from deep within, came the fractured but unmistakable tones of *Jingle Bells*.

The milk bar was a neat wooden structure set in the middle of a large asphalted car park and separated from the surrounding fields by grass verges and a low, dry-stone wall. Open countryside, bisected by the thin grey line of a minor road, rolled away on either side, losing itself in distant mist and nearer trees.

A sign at the car park entrance announced 'Closed till Easter'. In summertime both car park and countryside would be crawling with hikers, picnickers and sightseers. On a late December afternoon a solitary seagull strutted along the milk-bar's green-tiled roof. Alan pulled the BMW off the road and parked near the café entrance. He and Trevor climbed out, sniffing cautiously at the damp rural air.

It had been an interesting drive from the city. Trevor had preceded it by insisting on a complete change of clothes – a process that had involved him rummaging in a large store room at the rear of his office. He had clearly been using the place as a bedroom. And while Alan had prowled about with every sign of impatience he had been glad of the opportunity to look for evidence of female co-habitation. The fact that he spotted none was a source of uncertainty rather than reassurance. Had Charlotte moved out or had she never been here? If she had never been here did that mean she and Trevor had some other love nest?

Alan could, of course, simply have asked. But that would have meant surrendering some of his moral initiative which, for the moment at least, he was determined not to do – especially as Trevor's new wardrobe – a dark, thin-lapelled suit, a pale blue shirt and a cream, flashily patterned tie – seemed to restore much of his bumptiousness.

But Alan's buoyancy was reviving too, almost in spite of himself. Perhaps it was McCool's bizarre choice for the site of the final showdown in a place that had to be a good thirty miles from the nearest ice-cream van. Perhaps it was Trevor's exaggerated attempt to put on a good show, or simply the accumulated hysteria of a thoroughly traumatic week finally seeking its outlet – a week in which everything that could be done to him *had* been – at least twice.

Whatever the cause, as he and Trevor ambled across the rear of the car park, hilarity bubbled in Alan's veins, like nitrogen in a diver who has dived too deep for too long. Three or four wooden picnic tables and benches dotted the asphalt. Alan selected one and sat.

'I'm awfully glad we booked a table,' he commented.

Trevor began to pace up and down, slapping his arms together and stamping his feet. Neither man had bothered to bring an overcoat.

'He's a weird old bugger, picking a place like this.'

'What did he say on the telephone?' Alan asked.

'He said they do a nice lemon meringue pie here.'

Alan's hilarity saw its opening; the laughter emerged with explosive force. In a minute there were tears in the corners of his eyes. Suddenly the pressure had gone and the sheer bumbling absurdity of the whole fiasco was revealed to him.

'What's the joke?' Trevor scowled.

Alan waved a helpless hand. He was still giggling when a steel-grey Volvo saloon swung in off the road with a blast of its horn and eased to a halt next to the BMW. The driver's door opened and Mr McCool stepped out. He was dressed in a dark overcoat and a Homburg, plainly very much on his dignity.

He walked over, pulling on dark kid leather gloves.

'Hello, Trevor.'

'Hello, Uncle Luigi.'

This revelation tickled Alan even more; it was so beautifully consistent he could not have arranged it better himself. Somehow each further remark seemed calculated to fuel his giggles.

'How's your mother?' enquired Mr McCool.

'Very well,' said Trevor.

McCool reached a small paper bag out of his overcoat pocket. 'Would you like a sweetie?'

Alan howled.

The two ice-cream men regarded him, McCool guardedly, Trevor with a look of total mystification.

'Can we get down to business, Mr Bird, please?' McCool prompted, carefully re-pocketing his sweets.

With an effort Alan controlled himself. He rose from the picnic table and moved closer. 'You're Trevor's uncle?' he asked.

'That's right,' McCool agreed. Something of Alan's new assertiveness had communicated itself. McCool added, as if by way of appeasement: 'All the best families fight – you know that, Mr Bird.'

It was the note of complacency in the man's voice that finally got through to Alan. It neatly summarized an entire, uncaring attitude. Abruptly hilarity was no longer an adequate response. The anger that Alan had suppressed all week flashed into his eyes. 'Oh yes, I've heard that one a lot recently. Only I'm not family – and neither is my car!' He stabbed a finger in the direction of the Cabriolet standing shabbily in the shadow of the gleaming Volvo. 'And neither are any of those wonderful, freedom-loving, independent operators that you care about so deeply, Trevor. Have you any idea of the kind of games you've been playing? Never mind all the lies you've told me or the fortune you've cost me – or the fact that I've probably lost my job trying to help you – when neither of you was in the least bit interested in help!' He paused, red-faced, for breath. 'Well, whether you like it or not, I'm going to give you a chance to make it up. To me – to all those people that you've duped into believing in you. And to yourselves . . .' He pulled Katie Pollock's recipe from his jacket pocket, and held it up. 'You're going to work together on this – a joint venture.'

Trevor looked suspicious. 'What is it?' he asked.

'Ice-cream fritters,' Alan announced.

Trevor and McCool swapped glances. For a moment they were silent, then their lips began to curl. They started to laugh, low and scoffingly at first, then more heartily until both were coughing and spluttering. 'Alan,' McCool managed, 'you must be mad. *Matto!*'

'Now you can't afford to laugh!' Alan retaliated angrily. 'You're going to annihilate one another! This way you pool your resources. Your ice-cream –' he nodded at McCool '– and your deep-fry shops and trucks,' he told Trevor. 'You share a new product. Six hundred million Chinese can't be wrong.' He waved his slip of paper again. '*I* have the recipe.'

'Six hundred million Chinese . . .' McCool echoed, laughing again. But Trevor was nodding, persuaded to go along with the suggestion more as a continuation of the joke against Alan than out of any real conviction.

'Well,' he grinned, glancing at McCool who shrugged, 'we'll certainly give that a try, Dicky.'

'Trevor,' said Mr McCool, stifling his laughter, 'if you're willing, count me in . . .'

Still chuckling, uncle and nephew shook hands.

The tension showed in Alan's face. This seemed too swift, too easy. After a week of nightmare and sudden reversal he no longer trusted appearances of any kind.

'. . . And you promise you'll leave me alone – for ever and ever?' he persisted.

Trevor shrugged amicably. 'Sure!'

'Certainly, Dicky,' smiled Mr McCool, 'if that's what you want.'

'That's what I want,' Alan breathed.

They drove in procession, only pausing at the first telephone box so that Mr McCool could summon the rest of his clan. By the time they reached their destination – a smaller, more modern version of the McCool café on a busy suburban corner – Bruno, Paulo and Renato were skulking on the pavement outside. They exchanged curt, wary nods with Trevor as he rapped on the locked door.

Charlotte opened it.

She was dressed almost entirely in black: dark, skintight satin pants; a puffy-sleeved tunic top like the garb of a Renaissance prince; a black, loosely tied scarf. She seemed neither surprised nor pleased to see anyone.

Alan had wondered what his reaction might be when he saw her again, or hers to him. But as they filed into the Marinettis' premier fish and chip emporium it was the relationship between Charlotte and her brothers which absorbed him. He was aware of it immediately: a snarling, spitting antipathy, almost feral in its intensity, that threatened to spill into violence whenever they came within scratching distance of one another. It was unfortunate that all four, together with Trevor and Mr McCool, were obliged to squeeze into the same narrow space behind Alan in the shop's kitchen.

Self-interest, however, compelled a minimal degree of restraint. That and a growing desire to see precisely what Alan was about. For the first time he felt that he was acquiring the respect of the Bunnys and the McCools. As he whisked the ingredients of the batter with a brisk wrist action he was demonstrating the skill of a man who understood and appreciated food preparation almost as much as they did. Four years of enforced self-instruction, courtesy of Maddy, were finally paying off.

'There's something you'll appreciate at work here, Mr McCool,' he remarked. 'Perfect capitalism. We take one or two natural ingredients . . . the fruit of the earth – if you can call your ice-cream natural . . . we add the labour of man, his skill and ingenuity – and here is the secret bit –'

His audience strained forward as he lifted a

small brown packet from inside his jacket, tore off a corner and emptied the contents into his mixing bowl.

'And we create,' he beamed, whisking harder, 'a commodity which we sell at extreme profit to ourselves . . . Perfect, eh?'

He was conscious of McCool nodding distractedly, too intent to lift his eyes from the mixture. Alan finished whisking and turned toward a refrigerator chest to one side. Immediately there was a scrabbling motion behind him, harsh whispers between Charlotte and Bruno, and an unwrapped block of gold medal deluxe materialized beside him.

Carefully Alan sliced a portion off the end, lifted it with a spatula and immersed it swiftly in the batter mix. Then, holding his hand beneath the portion to catch the drops, he dashed toward the fryer at the front of the shop. His audience stampeded after him.

Transferring the ice-cream to a wire box, Alan lowered it into the hot fat. The others jostled around him as he counted off the seconds. At the right moment he lifted the box, shook it free of fat and eased the finished fritter on to a waiting plate.

He smiled with satisfaction, aware that the air of expectancy in the shop was now close to fever pitch. At least the fritter *looked* right. Light brown and crisp and approximately the right shape. Not at all bad for a first attempt.

Bodies were nudging his back as he cut it into neat cross-sections. The ice-cream interior still felt quite firm. He picked up a portion, pulling his arms out of the way as the others dived for their samples. A moment of earnest chewing followed.

'Hot!' Alan gasped, tonguing the mouthful away from his sensitive molar. 'And cold.' His face brightened. 'It's interesting, very, very interesting . . .'

'Bitter,' murmured Trevor, still tasting. 'And sweet . . .'

'Syrup,' said Mr McCool. 'It needs syrup. But the syrup would be extra – on the side – five, even ten pence a portion . . .'

Trevor was nodding. 'Thirty, forty pence for the fritter itself. Maybe more . . .'

'More, definitely more,' declared McCool. 'This is a luxury item. It needs a royal name.'

'King Fritter!'

McCool shook his head. 'That's too obvious.'

'We'd have to pre-cook and freeze-pack, then micro-heat at the point of sale . . .'

The excitement was building in Trevor's voice. McCool picked it up with a bout of fierce nodding. 'Hot ice-cream – year-round sales – summer and winter!'

Trevor began to laugh.

'It's a miracle!' McCool cried, joining him. 'It's a miracle!' Bellowing, they started to slap each other on the back.

'Hey, hey, hey!' Alan interrupted the jollity. 'Slow down – slow down. You haven't said if you liked it yet. Do you like it?'

'Oh it's a winner, Dicky!' Trevor beamed. Bruno patted him on the shoulder. 'Well done, Dicky!'

McCool was too excited to acknowledge the

interruption. His brain was moving into over-drive.

'Fifty per cent on the whole thing, Trevor – manufacture and sales. We'll have to equip the mobiles with micro-waves –'

'Paulo and I can handle the syrups, papa,' Bruno threw in. 'Maybe five or six flavours.'

'Flavours, yes!' McCool's eyes sparkled. 'Good boy, Bruno – you've got the syrups –'

Suddenly everyone, with the exception of Alan and Charlotte, who simply looked peeved, was tossing in suggestions. It was time for Alan to put this on the right footing.

'Slow down! Slow down!' he shouted over the hubbub. 'Look,' he said as it quietened, 'if you're talking business you ought to be talking to me.'

'Don't you worry, Dicky,' said Mr McCool quickly. 'We need a big campaign behind this one. We're revolutionizing the market. You can do the voice-overs.'

'Oh no, you don't understand,' Alan hurried on. 'You boys can run the show – that's fine. But I'm in for – what? – thirty per cent off the top.' He frowned. 'You could call that a consideration for having thought up the whole damned idea in the first place!' Now he had their fullest attention.

'Wait a minute,' said Trevor. 'You said you never wanted to see us again.'

'I don't,' said Alan. 'You can mail me the cheques.'

A pained look overtook McCool's features. For an awful moment Alan thought he was going to talk about honour again. 'But don't you just want to do the radio commercials, Dicky?' he tried.

'No,' said Alan flatly. 'And just in case you get

any fancy ideas, you won't find this in any cookery books.' He withdrew a second brown packet from inside his jacket. 'This is the batter adhesive agent. Without this you get a sticky, gooey mess, and the Chinese don't tell everybody about it.' He glimpsed a slow dawn of understanding in the eyes of Trevor and McCool. It was a sweet moment.

'So,' he smiled thinly, 'why don't we visit a lawyer on Monday morning and make this wonderful friendship legal? Oh – and one other item of mutual company expenditure – my car gets a complete repair job and a new roof. That way I might be persuaded to forget about charges of criminal damage and perhaps even breaking and entering one dark night recently. Okay?'

Trevor and McCool exchanged glances. There was an awkward silence. Abruptly Trevor's face broke into a broad grin. 'Yeah, sure, Dicky!' he cried.

Mr McCool nodded curtly; defeat came harder for him. 'Okay, *va bene*,' he said, and immediately launched into an animated discussion of product names. The others chimed in; suggestions surfaced from the babble of English and Italian: 'Bunny Frits!' 'Coolman Fritters!' 'Wafer Cools!'

It was Alan who silenced them all again. 'If you're looking for a name,' he said, 'what about "Dicky Fritters"?'

They all stared at him, blank looks on their faces as if they were uncertain whether he were making a serious suggestion, exercising his newfound power in some fresh way or both. Alan wasn't too sure himself, and frankly, at this stage, he no longer gave a damn.

Gingerly, taking care not to dislodge the dozens of tiny bulbs he had inserted under Maddy's direction, Alan was stripping his Christmas tree. Not completely, but enough to see the gaunt, natural shape underneath. From now on this would be an Alan Bird tree instead of a Madeleine Campbell tree, or a Madeleine Campbell-and-Alan tree. Lacking a little in colour and brilliance, perhaps, but a decent, unpretentious kind of a decoration. A decoration he could live with quite happily for the immediate future.

It was night outside as he worked, a sharp, wintry Glasgow night, fit only for staying out of, for finding somewhere snug and warm to sleep away the dark hours dreamlessly.

Somewhere out there, too, was Maddy. Telling her jokes, laughing at somebody else's, perhaps even now busy 'acquiring' something at a store foolish enough to stay open this late. But he doubted that.

The way his understanding of their relationship had deepened throughout the week still surprised him. He'd never thought himself that astute. He saw clearly, or clearly enough, the reasons for her criminal excursions – and the arguments that had preceded them – arguments he'd learned to live with, as he'd begun to live with her habit of 'acquisition', which, of course, was the very last thing she'd wanted.

All those little surprises had been intended to keep him on his toes, to keep the excitement, the uncertainty buzzing between them, to keep him the bright-eyed, twinkle-toed Dicky Bird he was for three short hours every morning and might even have been in reality when they'd first met four long years ago. Four years ago, but no more.

He got up, wincing at the cramp in his leg and winding the excess bulb wire around his hand.

Oh, excitement was still nice, he couldn't deny that, especially when provided by a woman as gorgeous as Maddy, or as stunning as his ice-cream queen. How close the two had been in his moment of triumph this afternoon. He'd seen it in Charlotte's eyes – that sudden look of surprise and appreciation and calculation – a transfer of allegiance from Trevor so blatant and so total it had lacked nothing but a signed and sealed affidavit. And all at once there was a Maddy who'd stepped back four, five, six years in time, ready to begin all over again . . .

Only he wasn't. He was a different flavour now. He was a mint chip when he'd been a raspberry ripple, or perhaps even a tutti frutti when the mood had taken him.

He grinned at the thought, bundled the lights and went to find room for them in the kitchen.

He didn't really know his new flavour. It might be months before he found out. And in the meantime he had a blank holiday Sunday to get through, scoffing what was left of his ice-cream and listening to Steve Kelly who'd drawn the short straw for the long Christmas afternoon stint. Could he dare invade the Semple family circle yet again?

But as he thought of Colin he remembered his

impromptu hospital visit and thought of Miss Wilson propped up in bed in her earphones eating NHS turkey. And suddenly a lot of things made a kind of sense.

He dropped the wires on the worktop, darted back into the living room and picked the telephone off the carpet. He dialled quickly.

'Oh Steve? Alan. Sorry to bother you this late . . .'

8

Christmas Day

Comfort and joy

'Well, it's three o'clock on this lovely peaceful Christmas afternoon and this is Dicky Bird being a very Happy Christmas Worm. You know, I got awfully sentimental after the morning show today, and I thought about poor old Steve Kelly having to come in here and spend the afternoon away from his lovely wife and gruesome kids – well, I'm only going by what Steve tells us: he's always saying they grew some more (sorry about that, Steve!). Anyway, batchelor boy Dicky volunteered!

'So here I am – I must be crackers, *matto*, crazy! But to tell you the truth we're having a pretty good time here in Metrosound today. There is definitely a party atmosphere – we've got the food, we've got the goodies and we've even got the odd drink or two, so don't feel too sorry for us . . .'

Alan faded up a Jim Reeves favourite as the

studio door opened. A lank-haired production assistant backed in with a steaming plastic cup of coffee in one hand and a paper plate in the other. Resting on the plate was one third of the individual Christmas pudding Alan had picked up on the way in. It was the last example of its kind he had been able to unearth in the deserted city, courtesy of the only Chinese supermarket in Hillhead. The plastic spoon which had been used to divide the spoils was still attached. Alan peered at it questioningly as the assistant put plate and cup on the edge of the console. Then he grinned and gave a thumbs up sign.

Through the control-room window he glimpsed the engineer chewing manfully. Three Christmas exiles. They were the sole occupants of the station.

Alan didn't mind. All that mattered was that a week of madness was over and he was back where he belonged, doing what he did best. And if it was hardly a deadly serious occupation, then at least it kept him safe from assault by iron bar or ice-cream cone. But he was no longer too sure what was truly serious and what was not. Bringing the tiniest spark of comfort, or even of joy, to the Miss Wilsons of this city, the Lily Semples, the proprietors of Chinese supermarkets, even – at a pinch – the Culinaris and the Marinettis, seemed, at the last, not at all trivial. In fact, the chance to do that, now he came to think of it, was worth an awful lot of ice-cream.

He reached for the fader.

'I hope you'll stay with us this afternoon and let us join your party, or if you haven't got a party of your own, you'll come and join ours. So, cheers everybody, everybody in this great big, weird and wonderful city of ours. I'm just going to sit back and play you some very nice music, talk my head off and tell you some of the worst jokes you're ever likely to repeat. And in the meantime, here's a little bit more of Mr Reeves while I tuck into my Christmas pud.'

He lifted the darkly glutinous mass from his plate and spooned it into his mouth in one go. It tasted almost exactly as he imagined a Chinaman's first attempt at this wholly British fare might. Absolutely awful.

'Mmmm,' Alan purred into the microphone, swallowing, along with the pudding, a sudden mad urge to giggle. 'Merry Christmas everybody. God bless us – every one!'